# The New Girl

Casey opened the car door. As she was about to step out, another car careened around the corner and swung into the space to her left, missing her door by about two inches.

"Hey!" Casey shouted. "Watch it next time! You nearly clipped me."

The other girl's dark eyes blazed as she got out of her silver BMW. "*You* watch it," she snarled at Casey. "That's my space you're parked in."

"Oh, yeah?" Casey folded her arms across her chest. "Show me your reserved sign."

The owner of the expensive silver car glared at Casey, then marched toward Thayer Hall. Casey burst out laughing—at herself. So much for her new dormmates being overawed by her.

She scooped up her three cartons of books and headed for the dorm. By the time she stepped off the elevator and into the third-floor hall, she couldn't wait to meet her new roommate. As Casey pushed the suite door open her face fell in surprise—standing there was the driver of the silver BMW.

"So, we meet again," Casey said. "I guess I'm about to crash your indoor parking space, too."

### NANCY DREW ON CAMPUS™

#1 New Lives, New Loves
#2 On Her Own
#3 Don't Look Back

Available from ARCHWAY Paperbacks

# Nancy Drew
## on campus ™ #3

# Don't Look Back

### Carolyn Keene

**AN ARCHWAY PAPERBACK**
Published by POCKET BOOKS
New York  London  Toronto  Sydney  Tokyo  Singapore

AN ARCHWAY PAPERBACK *Original*

An Archway Paperback published by
POCKET BOOKS, a division of Simon & Schuster Inc.
1230 Avenue of the Americas, New York, NY 10020

Copyright © 1995 by Simon & Schuster Inc.
Produced by Mega-Books, Inc.

ISBN: 0-671-52744-4

First Archway Paperback printing November 1995

10 9 8 7 6 5 4 3 2 1

NANCY DREW, AN ARCHWAY PAPERBACK and colophon are registered trademarks of Simon & Schuster Inc.

NANCY DREW ON CAMPUS is a trademark of Simon & Schuster Inc.

Cover photos by Pat Hill Studio

Printed in the U.S.A.

IL 8+

# Don't Look Back

# CHAPTER 1

Hey! Who's got the TV remote?" asked Nancy Drew's roommate, Kara Verbeck. She searched frantically under the cushions of the old couch that the freshmen in Suite 301 of Thayer Hall called the Black Hole. "It's almost time for *The President's Daughter*!"

"Better find it fast," Nancy said. "I think there's going to be a stampede."

As Nancy spoke, the doors to all the rooms in the suite were being yanked open. Barefoot, tousle-haired, and without makeup, the Wilder University freshmen had stopped whatever they were doing to hurry into the lounge they shared.

Nancy laughed. "I can't believe that all this excitement is over some old TV show," she said to Kara.

The expression on Kara's face suggested that Nancy must have just landed on campus from some distant—and totally hopeless—planet. "Some old TV show?" Kara echoed, her green eyes wide. "That's like calling the *Mona Lisa* some old painting."

The show in question was *The President's Daughter,* which had been the top-rated prime-time Sunday series for the previous four years. Now it was in reruns on Thursday nights at ten.

"I guess it is about time I watched *PD*," Nancy said to Kara. She picked up the remote from the top of the television set and handed it to her frazzled roommate.

The series had achieved cult status, and as her suitemates relived favorite scenes and tossed out *PD* trivia, Nancy was beginning to think that she was the only eighteen-year-old in America who hadn't seen a single episode.

Of course she had a pretty good excuse. Her boyfriend, Ned Nickerson, was at Emerson College while Nancy was back in River Heights. She'd spent a lot of Sunday evenings behind the wheel of her Mustang, driving home from visiting him.

Ned had expected Nancy to attend Emerson so they could be together, but she chose Wilder because of the school's top-notch journalism department. Nancy had decided to major in journalism, and Wilder's department easily beat out Emerson's.

An added bonus for choosing Wilder was that her two best friends, Bess Marvin and George Fayne, had decided to go there, too.

They all loved the beautiful old campus, with its towering oak trees and mix of modern and Gothic architecture. The place combined the best of the old with that of the new. Wilder definitely felt alive with possibilities—new ideas and new people.

"Oooh, this is one of my favorites!" Reva Ross exclaimed from the other side of Kara, bringing Nancy back to the present. Reva, one of the smartest of Nancy's suitemates, grabbed her long black hair and pulled it away from her sculpted, dusky face. "It's the episode where the president's daughter is stalked by a psycho. When I saw it for the first time, I couldn't even watch the scene where—"

"Wait, Reva! Don't tell me," Nancy interrupted. "I haven't seen it yet, remember?"

"Well, just prepare to bite your nails." Reva shivered in anticipation.

Nancy laughed and leaned back comfortably against a throw pillow, settling in to watch the show.

"Really, Reva," a languid voice said. "Nancy never does anything as unwholesome as bite her nails." A dark head of hair belonging to the voice moved into Nancy's line of sight just as the show began.

"Down in front," Nancy said, annoyance creeping into her voice as she realized who was blocking her view.

"Well, excu-use me," Stephanie Keats drawled. Tall and striking in a frankly contrived way, her pale skin was set off by expensively cut dark hair. She made no attempt to move out of Nancy's way.

"You make a better door than a window, Stephanie," Nancy said as she moved over to sit next to Eileen O'Connor, one of her more easygoing suitemates. Nancy blew away an annoying wisp of hair that had tumbled across her face. She wasn't going to let Stephanie ruin her evening.

Nancy knew that Stephanie went out of her way to make her life miserable. Before private phones were installed in the students' rooms, Stephanie had managed repeatedly to "forget" to tell Nancy about Ned's phone calls on the lounge phone.

Ned . . .

Her boyfriend . . . ex-boyfriend, Nancy reminded herself.

Deep down Nancy knew that a big part of Wilder's allure had been that it *wasn't* Ned's school. Emerson was already so familiar to her. If she had gone there, she would have ended up hanging out with Ned and his friends, going to their favorite spots, and taking intro courses they had already taken. She had wanted to go someplace she could make her own, someplace she could discover for herself.

Nancy didn't regret her decision. Wilder was everything she had hoped it would be. She didn't expect that choosing Wilder over Emerson would lead to her breakup with Ned, though.

Had she really broken up with him?

Her first and only true love?

Forever?

"Yo, Nancy. Anybody home? It's starting." Eileen was moving her hand up and down in front of Nancy's face to get her attention. "The TV set's thataway. Hello?"

Nancy put her thoughts of Ned aside. What she had heard about the show sounded good. She thought *PD* sounded like an interesting show with a mix of fun, outrageous plots, and, once in a while, a serious episode like that of the stalker.

The best part of watching the show was that it was part of her latest assignment for the *Wilder Times,* the college newspaper.

Casey Fontaine, the actress who played the president's daughter on the show, was now a freshman at Wilder. Nancy was supposed to interview her and write a short profile. She hoped that this profile of Wilder's most famous freshman would get her more work in the future.

Nancy was just a rookie on the paper, and she had to pay her dues writing captions and blurbs about school clubs and events. Nancy had been disappointed when Gail Gardeski, the editor of the *Wilder Times,* had rewritten her first important piece for the paper, an interview with the team's quarterback. It had been her own fault, though, because she'd handed in the assignment late.

This time Nancy planned on getting her article in early. It wasn't due till Monday afternoon. Nancy had already done a lot of the research, collecting articles about Casey from the Wilder library's extensive magazine collection, but she still hadn't seen the young actress in action.

"You'll love Casey," Nancy's friend Bess had told her when she'd learned of Nancy's assignment. Bess had made friends with the actress during rehearsals for the musical *Grease!,* which was set to be the first production of Wilder's theater department that year. Bess and Casey both had parts in the show.

As the opening credits rolled over freeze-frame shots of the stars, Nancy zeroed in on Casey Fontaine's face. Caught by the camera in the middle of a laugh, her head thrown back and her waist-length red hair flying, Casey's TV character was undeniably appealing. Fresh-faced and mischievous-looking, young and sophisticated at the same time, she was the girl next door until she wound up at the White House.

The young actress's face gave way to the athletic but soulful handsomeness of Charley Stern. He played a college newspaper reporter who'd talked his way into the White House press corps and then had fallen in love with Casey's character, Ginger Porter.

Groans and sighs rose up around Nancy.

"Save me from drowning." Eileen sighed loudly. "Isn't he gorgeous?"

Nancy hoped that Eileen and her other suitemates were too caught up in their own emotions to notice hers. Charley Stern was more than just another gorgeous actor. Something about him reminded Nancy of Peter Goodwin, a handsome Wilder junior who also lived in Thayer.

Peter made Nancy feel things she had felt only for Ned in the past. While it was thrilling, it was also confusing. How could she be so attracted to someone so soon after breaking up with Ned?

She tried to deny her feelings for Peter, and succeeded sometimes, but as soon as she saw Peter again, she felt herself falling for him.

It wasn't only her memories of Ned that complicated things between her and Peter. Peter had just broken up with Dawn Steiger, the resident adviser for Nancy's suite, and it was obvious to everyone that Dawn was still in love with Peter. Would Nancy be risking her friendship with Dawn by pursuing Peter?

One other thing nagged at Nancy. Dawn had hinted on more than one occasion that Peter was carrying some serious baggage from the past. But she never elaborated on it. Nancy wondered what that could be and if she'd ever know the handsome premed student well enough to find out.

"If Charley Stern actually visits Casey on campus, I may have to lock myself in my room," Reva declared. "Otherwise I might make a total fool of myself."

"I thought Charley and Casey were history," Eileen said.

"Yeah, I was looking at a tabloid paper while I was waiting in line at the supermarket this summer, and I saw a story about them," Liz Bader said. "The story said that Casey was in London, shopping for new clothes for college, while Charley did the club scene in New York with one of the teen stars from a daytime soap opera."

"I don't think they've broken up," Ginny Yuen argued. "I just saw a photo spread of them in *TV Guide*. Casey and Charley were surfing on location in Hawaii, and they were together at a black-tie Hollywood opening."

Nancy was getting to be an expert on Casey Fontaine because of her research, and one thing she had learned was that she couldn't believe everything she read. She knew that some reporters didn't even speak to the people they wrote about. Instead, they based their articles on rumor and gossip. They were more interested in selling their stories than in telling the truth. They so often got their facts wrong that Nancy wondered if they did it on purpose to make their articles more exciting. That was why her interview with Casey was crucial to doing a good job on this assignment. She wanted to get the facts straight.

Nancy watched the show closely, analyzing Casey's work. Within the space of a few minutes, Casey's character, Ginger Porter, provoked laughter, sympathy, a romantic shiver, and a spine-tingling shudder of fear. Nancy was impressed. Casey was definitely a talented actress.

"I know how Ginger feels," Liz said. "I once got followed home by a guy who'd seen me on the subway. If my doorman hadn't sent him away, I could have been in real trouble." Liz, a street-smart New Yorker, was Ginny's roommate.

Nancy tried to block out her suitemates' conversation. They'd all seen this episode before, but she had to concentrate on the plot.

"We have our very own Secret Service— campus security," Stephanie drawled. "They'd probably welcome the excitement of tracking down a stalker. I mean, who wouldn't?" She yawned.

Liz tore into a bag of gourmet potato chips. She took a couple and passed the bag to Nancy. Nancy started to shake her head, then took a few, and passed the bag along to Eileen.

Eileen began to read the nutritional information on the package. "No fat, no salt—"

"No taste," interrupted Ginny, who was chewing on one. she made a face. "It's like eating cardboard. Want one, Stephanie?"

"Potato chips? No, thank you." Stephanie wrinkled her nose. "Whenever Julie had the munchies, the room would reek of potato chips. Oh, the blessings of living in a single."

Nancy was finding it too hard to concentrate on the show. She'd try to get videotapes to watch by herself. The conversation was distracting her.

"Has anyone heard from Julie Hammerman?" Ginny asked.

"Dawn went to visit her last week, I think," Eileen said.

"Well, I hope Dawn didn't 'lose' anything while she was there," Stephanie said, raising her eyebrows.

Julie had been Stephanie's roommate when college started. Her suitemates discovered Julie had a serious drug problem when she'd stolen from all of them to get money to buy drugs. Nancy and some of the girls had caught her. Instead of going to jail, Julie had been sent to a nearby rehab clinic.

The girls in the suite were pretty angry at Julie, but when they found out about her drug problem, they became more sympathetic. Julie was paying big dues: Her college career was in pieces, and now she was living behind locked doors. Only Stephanie still knocked her.

Liz offered her the bag of chips to Reva. "I don't know who Julie's rooming with in rehab," she said to Stephanie, "but Julie may think the scenery's improved, too."

"Pipe down, guys, the show's starting again," Eileen commanded.

Just then Dawn came into the lounge, a grin on her face. "I just got some big news," she said in a loud voice. "Guess who's moving into Thayer 301 tomorrow!"

Nancy noticed that Stephanie's shoulders visibly stiffened. Hers was the only room in the suite with an empty bed.

Dawn waited a moment to create suspense before announcing, "Casey Fontaine!"

# CHAPTER 2

Book in hand, Casey Fontaine curled up on her sea green quilted satin coverlet. Elegant enough for a Hollywood boudoir but as comforting as a baby blanket, it was the one luxury she allowed herself as a freshman at Wilder.

Casey was careful not to flaunt her fame or wealth. She just wanted to blend in with the other college freshmen.

A window open to let in the soft night air of early autumn let her hear the theme music from *The President's Daughter*. The young actress was well aware that while she was intent on the pages of *Jane Eyre*, most of her classmates were focusing on her face.

Except that it wasn't *her* face, she thought, glancing in the mirror. It was her character's. She'd cut her hair short before starting college because she wanted everyone to know that she was Casey Fontaine, not Ginger Porter.

Casey's roommate, Elissa, burst through the door and tossed her backpack on her bed. "But, Ginger," she began, hamming it up. "How can you be here when you're in the White House?" She gestured dramatically at the miniature pink TV on Casey's desk, making her point even though the set was turned off.

Casey laughed at Elissa's teasing. Her roommate knew how it annoyed Casey to be mistaken for her TV character.

Ginger had been fun to play—double fun when Casey had fallen in love with Charley. But Ginger was a kid, and Casey was tired of being a kid. She was tired of playing the president's plucky but scatterbrained daughter.

"I'm a college woman now," she said to Elissa, liking the sound of the phrase. It had been a tough decision to leave the show and Hollywood and Charley, but now she was glad she had, and not just because her parents had insisted.

Mr. and Mrs. Fontaine had wanted their daughter to go to college because the Hollywood club scene made them nervous. Casey had wanted to go to college because her parents made her nervous. They constantly moaned that stardom had deprived Casey of a normal adolescence, but *they* were the chief deprivers. Whenever she ate dessert, they fretted that she'd look fat on camera. When she skipped a meal, they worried that she was anorexic. If she slept fewer than eight hours a night, they delivered a lecture on her getting run-down. If she slept more than nine hours, they fussed about burnout and depression. During the period when she'd dated lots of guys, they'd complained that she was running wild. Then when she'd started dating Charley exclusively, they said she was getting too serious too soon.

Sure, they loved her, and Casey loved them, but it felt really good to be on her own. They were always hovering in the background, making sure that she wasn't being exploited. But Casey didn't think she needed their protection. Except maybe from one particular reporter. Just thinking about him made Casey shudder.

Gavin Michaels worked for the *Hollywood Star,* a supermarket tabloid that was obsessed with TV and movie stars as well as the occasional UFO sighting. Gavin had been hounding Casey the month before she left the show to go to college, because Casey's agent refused to grant him an interview. Once he even sneaked into her trailer on the studio lot, and she'd caught him going through her stuff. After that, security was tightened and Gavin was banished from the lot.

If only he could have been banished from my life, thought Casey.

Yes, it felt doubly good to be away from California, even though it meant being separated from Charley. Casey loved Charley, and she knew he loved her. But a lot could happen when two people were separated, especially if one of them was still a TV star living in Hollywood and the other an ex–TV star now in her first year of college.

Originally Mr. and Mrs. Fontaine had planned to move back to their hometown of Springdale, half an hour from Wilder, but then they'd been offered a chance to buy the Hollywood Hills shoe salon they managed. They hadn't been able to resist. Thank heavens! She got along much better with her parents when they were more than a thousand miles away.

"So what happened to packing?" Elissa's eyes brightened. "Tell me you've changed your mind about moving."

"I wish," Casey said sincerely. "I'm going to miss you, Elissa. But—" Her thought was punctuated by a loud sneeze. Grabbing a tissue from the family-size box next to her bed, she blew her nose. "It seems that I just can't live in a hundred-year-old building. Shots or no shots," she added, rubbing her arm where she'd gotten injections to help deal with her severe allergy to dust.

"I'll vacuum under my bed every day,"

Elissa offered, as if they hadn't had this conversation a dozen times a day since Casey had told her she was moving. "I'll give away all my fuzzy sweaters."

Casey laughed affectionately. "You're such a dream roommate, Elissa," she said. "I wish I could take you with me. I'll bet my new roommate won't be half as much fun as you are. And I'm sure my new room won't have anywhere near as much charm," she added, taking in the faded but appealing violet-sprigged wallpaper.

The phone rang. Both girls eyed the white instrument, perched precariously on Casey's messy desk.

"Charley?" Elissa said.

Casey shrugged and grabbed the handset. "Hello?" There was no answer. "Hello?" she said again, then quickly hung up.

"Our mystery caller again?" Elissa asked.

Casey nodded as a shiver snaked its way up her back, but she was actress enough to keep from showing what she felt.

Someone had been calling Casey and Elissa's room once or twice a day since the beginning of school. Whoever it was always hung up without saying a word. Elissa figured it was some starstruck student who got a thrill from calling Casey's number. But Casey wasn't so sure.

"Well, if you're determined to move, I might

as well help you." Elissa picked up one of the cardboard cartons that were stacked in a corner. "Let's start with your desk. Then we'll know the worst is behind us."

"You do my sneakers, I'll do the desk," Casey said quickly, relieved to be able to think about something else.

She didn't want anyone, not even Elissa, whom she trusted more than anyone else at Wilder, to see the thick folder of letters in the second drawer of her desk. She couldn't throw them out, but she couldn't share them, either. Not if she wanted to be allowed to stay at Wilder.

She'd received weird fan letters before, but the ones she'd started getting in California last year were creepier than usual. They were more like love letters than fan mail. The writer was obviously obsessed with her, and the letters were getting more and more intimate. What was really creepy, though, was that whoever was writing the letters seemed to know a lot about her.

Casey had hoped that when she started at Wilder, the letters would stop. But it wasn't exactly a secret that she was attending Wilder. Anyone could easily have found out her new address. And someone who professed his love in almost daily letters wouldn't be put off too easily, Casey figured.

Much as she hated to admit the parallel, her

predicament was as disturbing as Ginger's in that night's episode of *PD*. But unlike Ginger, Casey didn't have Secret Service protection or Charley's TV character to save her.

Casey took a deep breath and tried to calm her too rapidly beating heart. No, it's not the same, she reminded herself. Her letters weren't threatening. If they had been, she would have gotten protection. And if she seriously thought she was in danger, of course she would go to the police.

There was another reason Casey hesitated to report the letters to the police.

Her parents.

She knew they would hire bodyguards to trail her to classes. They'd probably even tell them to wait outside the bathroom while Casey brushed her teeth.

Well, there was one good thing about her move to Thayer. The modern dorm didn't have the antique charm of Wallace House, but security was a lot tighter.

She hoped it was tight enough.

Bess Marvin vigorously shook her blond head, willing herself to stay awake as Professor Lockhart droned on and on about the gradual collapse of the Roman Empire.

This was Western Civ, she reminded herself—not Introductory Physics. So why did her eyelids seem to weigh five pounds apiece, as if they were part of a science project demonstrating the relentless law of gravity?

Firmly grasping her purple felt-tip pen, Bess forced herself to jot down the professor's words on the lined paper in front of her.

Mmm, it would be so nice to stretch out and sleep under one of the oak trees that dotted the campus. . . .

The next thing she knew, her pen had tumbled to the floor with what sounded like a thunderous clatter. As her head jerked up, she realized to her hideous embarrassment that she'd fallen asleep. She'd been out for only a moment, but she was sure her head had lolled forward noticeably.

As Bess bent to pick up her pen, she almost brushed against the denim-clad leg of the guy sitting next to her. This was not just any guy—this was an incredibly cute guy. Mickey somebody-or-other. Bess noticed he was wearing mismatched red socks. One was definitely darker than the other.

She could almost hear the voice of her ultra-grind roommate, Leslie King. "If you paid half as much attention to your academic work as you do to guys' socks, you might bring your average soaring to a C minus." Leslie, the human ice cube, who never missed an opportunity to put Bess down because Bess chose to enjoy life instead of spending every free moment studying.

For the millionth time since she'd arrived at Wilder, Bess wished she were rooming with Nancy and George. She had wanted the three of them to try for a triple, but apparently she was the only one who wanted that.

As the tall, gray-haired professor droned on about the Visigoths, Bess wondered if it was her fault that her courses were less interesting than Mickey's socks.

Besides, the only reason she was in this class at all was because she'd gotten to registration a little late and then stood in the wrong line. By the time it was her turn to register, all the good classes were taken, including the one Bess wanted most, Drama 101.

Next semester she'd be at the head of the line. At least she was learning from her mistakes.

Unfortunately her mistakes weren't limited to taking the wrong classes. Western Civ was nothing compared to her biggest mistake so far—letting a guy she hardly knew corner her at his frat house.

At first Dave Cantera had seemed like a nice guy. When he offered to give her a tour of the Zeta house during a frat party, she agreed, not realizing he was just using that as an excuse to make a beeline for his room, on the second floor. Remembering the smell of beer on Dave's breath and the leer in his bloodshot eyes as he moved in on her in his room, Bess shuddered in the overheated classroom.

What had made the experience even worse was that she had had to cope with it on her own. Nancy and George were so busy with their own lives that it was days before she even had a chance to confide in her best friends—long days when Bess was close to tears most of the time.

No, her two friends weren't there for Bess the way they would have been when they were in high school. Back then, they did everything together, but now they were all leading separate lives. She missed being around her two best friends.

"Ms. Marvin?"

The sound of her own name startled Bess. She realized to her horror that Professor Lockhart had asked her a question.

"Excuse me?" she blurted out. Someone behind her snickered, and Bess wished that the floor would open up and suck her down.

"Thank you, Ms. Marvin," the professor said acidly. "You just answered the question. What destroyed the Roman Empire was the *indifference* of its inhabitants. They didn't really care. They didn't pay attention. Enjoy the weekend, ladies and gentlemen, but not in excess," he added. The professor always concluded his Friday lecture with those words.

Cheeks burning as though they'd been

slapped, Bess shoved her notebook into her backpack and rushed out of the classroom. She knew she was going to cry—no way she could keep the tears from coming—but she wasn't going to give Professor Hardheart the satisfaction of seeing her break down.

By the time Bess made it back to her room, she already had tears standing in her eyes. At least she was alone—Leslie was probably at a study group. After grabbing a tissue, Bess wiped her eyes and blew her nose. She knew she didn't look her best, even without a red nose and tear-stained cheeks. Last night's round of parties—on top of the parties the night before—had taken its toll on her looks. Feeling the sting of salt in her eyes, she knew she was going to look like absolute hell when she finally did stop crying, and that just made her cry harder.

This was a very important day, one that might make all the difference in her life at Wilder. That afternoon Bess had another round of sorority rush parties. She was scheduled to visit six, ending up at Kappa, the house where she most wanted to pledge.

Nancy and George had decided against rushing. Nancy had the newspaper, and George was more interested in athletics than rush parties.

Of course, Bess reminded herself, I have the drama department. She thought of the role she had in the chorus of *Grease!*, where she was making new friends, like Brian Daglian, who had been her scene study partner for the auditions, and of course Casey Fontaine.

Bess hoped she'd be in all the college productions—even if only backstage. That was another thing she had in common with the girls she hoped would become her sorority sisters. Lots of the Kappas were interested in the arts as she was, and most of them had been warm and friendly on her preliminary visits. That was no guarantee they would invite her to pledge, however, and it wouldn't help her chances if she showed up all droopy and red eyed.

She needed to get changed, and not just for the rush parties. She had a rehearsal for *Grease!* later, and she wanted to look her best for that, too.

Bess stared at her face in the mirror. "Chin up, Marvin," she said to her reflection. "Stop feeling sorry for yourself." The tear-stained, red-eyed image that looked back at her told her she'd better do something to fix her face. Suddenly Bess had an idea.

Bess flopped onto her bed facedown, reached under the flower-patterned dust ruffle, and pulled out dozens of glossy magazines. (Who said she wasn't organized?) Impatiently tossing aside one publication after the other, she finally found the article she was looking for: "The Beauty Salon in Your Refrigerator."

Bess began to read. "To bring out the luster in tired hair, try combing it through with mayonnaise. . . . Rest your elbows in grapefruit halves. . . . Mashed avocado makes a soothing facial mask. . . . Slices of cucumber placed over the eyes can take away redness and puffiness in fifteen relaxing minutes. . . ."

"That's it!" Bess said out loud as she hurried to the communal refrigerator in the lounge at the end of the hall. Pulling open the produce drawer, Bess silently vowed never again to make fun of the two skinny dance majors in Room 224 who kept it stocked with carrots, lettuce, peppers, and shiny cucumbers. She scribbled a note on a paper towel: "I.O.U. a cuke. Bess M."

Returning to her room, she noticed that when she was rummaging on her desk, more than just the magazine had tumbled to the floor. Her side of the room looked as if a tornado had hit. Leslie would not be pleased when she got back. Messiness distracted Leslie from studying.

But there was no time to clean up now. Tomorrow would be clean-up day, as well as cucumber replacement day, and maybe even hit-the-books day, Bess promised herself. She also had to write a letter home and balance her checkbook.

Now she needed a few minutes of beauty rest. Bess put on a CD of her favorite rock group, lay down on her bed, and placed the cucumber slices over her eyes.

All those boring chores could wait till tomorrow. Today she had parties and a rehearsal to go to, and she wanted to do both looking her best.

# CHAPTER 3

The man sat in his car across from the Thayer parking lot. He had purposely parked in the shade so the shadows would conceal him from her.

Soon there would be no need to hide from his love. But he wasn't quite ready yet.

"Soon . . ." he whispered, gazing across at the one and only love of his life, Casey Fontaine.

He had loved her for years. He knew he would love her forever. Theirs was the kind of love that went beyond this world.

What's this? he thought as he watched her carrying boxes out the door and piling them into her car.

She wasn't leaving college, was she? So soon?

Please don't leave me, he silently begged. Please, please promise you'll never leave me again.

Her gaze seemed to drift his way, and he willed himself to be invisible inside the car.

Daring to turn back toward her, he watched as she piled suitcases on top of the boxes in the backseat of the little white car.

"Please," he begged again, this time out loud. "Please let her be moving somewhere nearby."

The car was a beauty, just like her. And easy to spot and follow.

He could stay a few cars back on the highway and still keep her in sight.

He loved her so much that just the sight of her with her new cute short haircut behind the wheel of her MG sent his pulse racing. He had to hold himself back from rushing his plan.

Patience, he silently reminded himself. They had an eternity to spend together.

As she started her engine and pulled away from the curb with a stylish roar, he looked at his gas gauge. Full. He congratulated himself on being so well prepared. And he had his credit card in his wallet, right?

It didn't matter where she was going.

Whatever road she took, he would be right behind her, until the day when they would be together—forever.

\* \* \*

George Fayne and Will Blackfeather were standing at the kitchen counter in the off-campus apartment Will shared with Andy Rodriguez. They both stared at a package as they sipped glasses of orange juice.

"I can't wait any longer," George said, moving toward the package.

"Me, either," said Will.

Without ceremony, they ripped open the brown paper in which someone at the campus publications office had neatly wrapped a hundred posters announcing the first meeting of Earthworks, an environmental action group they were active in.

The cartoonish posters featured neon-bright bottles and cans with human features in shades of green from lime to pine. George and Will had designed the poster, and an art major had done the drawing.

"Awesome," George said, privately thinking that the word suited Will even better than it did the poster. With his coppery skin, dark hair, and a lean frame that exuded energy, he shook her up every time she took a close look at him. Which was as often as she could manage.

"They're great!" Will pronounced, then looked at George and said quietly, *"You're great."*

To her dismay, George felt her face turning red.

28

"You're blushing," Will said, his eyes bright with amusement.

"I am not," George said with dignity.

Will's almond-shaped eyes flickered over her still pink face. "We work well together." His fingertips traced the path his eyes had taken.

George came down with a sudden case of shaky knees. The unsteady feeling made her want to do two opposite things. Half of her wanted to sink down on the corduroy couch in Will's living area wrapped in his arms. The other half wanted to run a five-minute mile out the front door and up the hill toward her dorm. Alone. Sometimes the intensity of her feelings for Will scared her.

She chose a compromise. "Let's start putting the posters up around campus," she suggested.

"Okay," Will agreed. Carefully setting the posters inside his leather backpack, he added, "But the truth is, I'd rather kiss you than save the environment. Dedicated activist though I am."

George felt as giddy and breathless as though she'd just done a high jump. "What about saving the environment first, then kissing me," she suggested. "That can be our reward to ourselves, extra kissing."

Will slung his backpack over one shoulder, then cupped George's face in his hands.

"You've just made the most important advance in political activism since the invention of the printing press," he said. "I think that deserves a reward all its own."

Will looked into her eyes and brought his lips down on hers. George felt a rush of pleasure, and her mind filled with the sound of his name: Will.

She had never felt happier in her entire life.

Casey Fontaine downshifted the vintage white MG, sending gravel spinning as she swung into the parking lot behind Thayer and came to a stop.

She turned off the ignition, patting the warm dashboard as the engine ticked down, then softly purred before becoming silent. It responded to her moods—at least it seemed to. She prided herself on being able to interpret its various sounds.

This particular purr, for instance, meant "Feed me." The gas gauge said Full, but Casey wasn't fooled. It was the one unreliable dial on the dashboard.

She dropped her key ring into her pocket but made no move to open the door. Her stomach suddenly felt tight and hollow, as if the lights had come on and the cameras were rolling.

Casey Fontaine nervous about moving into a college dorm? Who'd believe it? She'd spent a night at the White House as the guest of the real-life president's daughter. She'd gone to a garden party at Buckingham Palace and met the queen. After all, she was a certified star, and it was the other girls who were supposed to be uptight about how to deal with her. So why was she the one with the butterflies?

That was the thing to do, she realized, focus on the other kids' anxiety. Try to get them to relax, she told herself, and she was sure to relax herself in the process.

"So come on, Casey. Open the door," she murmured.

But she couldn't. Maybe what she was anxious about had nothing to do with the other kids. Maybe it had to do with that creepy feeling that someone was watching her. A feeling she'd been having all too often since she got to Wilder. Once or twice she could have sworn a black car was following her. But then, there were so many black cars around, she could have been mistaken. Still . . .

Just as she was beginning to freak out, Casey got a grip. Being an actress was about being watched, right? On screen and stage and off, too. It went with the territory.

Casey made herself focus on the Y-shaped building in front of her. Big, sleek, and modern, it had a decidedly urban feel to it with its black window frames filled with natural-colored shades. Casey remembered the front entrance she had passed on her way to the back parking lot. The shiny brass columns and huge glass doors made Thayer Hall look a little like a luxury hotel. Maybe it would swallow her up the way Los Angeles and New York did, letting her melt into the crowd.

Yes, the move to Thayer had definitely been smart, even though she'd miss Elissa. And Thayer was the newest dorm on campus. Not much dust could have accumulated yet, Casey hoped.

Drawing a deep breath, she opened the car door. As she was about to step out, a car careened around a corner of the lot, going much too fast.

Casey screamed as the car bore down on her.

"No" Bess tried to shout. "No!" But the word was trapped in her throat; she couldn't get a sound out. Dave held her tightly as she struggled to get away. His face loomed inches from hers, his drunken laughter reverberating in her ears. . . .

"Bess! Wake up!"

"Wha— where?" Bess awoke feeling disoriented. It took her a moment to realize that she was in her dorm room in Jamison and the hand shaking her shoulder belonged to her roommate, Leslie King. Bess sighed. That night with Dave Cantera was still intruding on her dreams.

Bess blinked her eyes—or tried to. Why

were her eyelids so heavy? Then she remembered the cucumber slices. Peeling them off, she sighed with relief. Then she saw the clock.

"Oh, no!" She had only twenty minutes until she was due at the first of the sororities on her rush party schedule, and she hadn't even washed her hair yet!

"Looks like you're getting ready to dig in for another big night of studying," Leslie commented sarcastically as Bess grabbed her terry-cloth robe and towel.

Bess was in no mood for Leslie's all-work-and-no-play attitude, and for once she wasn't going to take it. "You know, Leslie, you can learn some things from living life instead of reading about it," she returned.

Settling down at her perfectly organized desk, Leslie rolled her eyes at Bess. "I didn't realize that Partying 101 was a freshman requirement. When does it meet, Bess? Every day from five till midnight?"

"I'm not *just* going to parties." Bess hated it when Leslie put her on the defensive. "I've got a theater rehearsal, too. Even premeds must have some appreciation for the arts."

"Come on, Bess." Leslie straightened a stray piece of paper on her desk. "You've got a bit part in a college musical production. It's hardly a major cultural event. Speaking of art, didn't you say you had a paper on the Renaissance due Tuesday?" Leslie said casually.

"Monday," Bess muttered, trying to hide a flutter of panic. She wasn't going to give Leslie the satisfaction of hearing her admit it, but she knew she really had to buckle down—and soon.

Tomorrow, she promised herself as she raced toward the shower. Tomorrow I'll go to the library, no matter what. Unless something better comes up . . .

Casey cowered as the car swung into the space to her left, missing her door by two inches. Her momentary panic changed to fury as the driver of the silver BMW got out.

She was a tall girl with an arrogant scowl that marred her otherwise pretty pale face.

"Hey!" Casey shouted. "Watch it next time! You nearly clipped me."

The other girl's dark eyes blazed. "*You* watch it," she snarled at Casey. "That's my space you're parked in."

"Oh, yeah?" Casey folded her arms across her chest. "Show me your reserved sign."

The owner of the expensive silver car glared at Casey but didn't say anything. Flinging her jacket and bag over her shoulder, she marched toward Thayer in a silence that spoke louder than words.

Casey burst out laughing—at herself. So much for her new dormmates being overawed by her. But maybe she would be lucky and the other girl would live on a different floor.

She drew a deep breath and scooped up three cartons of paperback books.

Nancy was heading into the dorm with a pile of borrowed *President's Daughter* videotapes when she saw what appeared to be a stack of cartons on human legs. The legs ended in sparkling gold high-top sneakers.

Then one of the cartons started to slide, and Nancy ran forward to grab it. As the weight of the heavy box shifted into her arms, she saw the face that went with the legs and closely cropped red hair.

Casey Fontaine! What luck. Now Nancy could make a date to interview her.

"Casey, welcome to Thayer," she said. "I'm Nancy Drew. I left a message on your machine at your old dorm about interviewing you for the *Wilder Times*."

"Sure, I remember. Hi, and thanks for the help." Casey grinned behind her heavy load. "I guess my reputation is in your hands as well as my carton. Do you live in Thayer? I'm looking for Suite 301. Maybe you could point me in the right direction."

"I'm going there right now," Nancy said. "I'm one of your suitemates, actually." Nancy reached for another carton as she spoke, but Casey shook her head.

"I'm fine with these," Casey said. "You got the heavy one."

"You know, we have a friend in common, Bess Marvin," Nancy said as she led the way into an elevator.

"That's right, she's mentioned you a bunch of times. I love Bess," Casey declared. "She's so warm and bubbly. And when you talk to her, she really listens. I don't think she has a mean bone in her body."

"She doesn't," Nancy agreed, shifting the box from one arm to the other. Talking about Bess reminded Nancy that she hadn't been spending much time with her friend lately.

"Which is more than I can say about some people around here," Casey continued. The two girls stepped off the elevator and into the third-floor hall. "Down in the parking lot, I met this—well, this *shark*. Oh, is this it?" she added as Nancy stopped.

The suite door swung open. Nancy looked on as Casey and Stephanie stared at each other. She could tell that neither girl liked what she saw.

Casey broke the silence. "So, we meet again. I guess I'm about to crash your indoor parking space, too."

# CHAPTER 4

The pleasant Victorian building that housed Kappa was starting to feel like home, Bess realized happily. Everyone seemed to know her name and have a welcoming word.

"Hi, Bess."

"Bess Marvin! Nice to see you."

"Great beads, Bess. Like Venetian glass. How are the *Grease!* rehearsals going?"

Well, *almost* everyone was friendly. Soozie Beckerman seemed to have had it in for Bess from the moment they'd met. Now, looking at Soozie dressed in unrelieved black, Bess felt like cotton candy in her oversize pink silk shirt and matching leggings.

"Where's Casey?" Soozie asked. Her tone of voice made Bess feel like a gate-crasher.

So Casey was the price of admission to

Kappa, Bess realized with a pang of nervousness. Of course no one had actually come right out and told her that.

"I just assumed you would bring her," Soozie went on, "but then maybe you two aren't quite as tight as you've let on."

Bess felt her cheeks grow hot. She liked Casey as a person, but she would die of embarrassment if the actress—or anyone else—thought Bess was showing off their friendship.

Fortunately, Holly Thornton came to Bess's rescue. The easygoing blond vice president of Kappa liked Bess and seemed as determined to smooth Bess's way into the sorority as Soozie was to put out stumbling blocks.

"We all think Casey would be an asset to Kappa," Holly said lightly. "And I'm sure she'd accept an invitation to pledge here if she were going to pledge anywhere. But hard as it is to believe, Soozie, there's more to life than the Greeks."

Soozie raised her perfect eyebrows. "Is that what you're planning to tell our visitors?" she asked challengingly, gesturing at the living room crowded with groups of girls chatting, sipping tea from china cups, and nibbling sandwiches and cakes. "You hardly sound like a Kappa officer."

"Are you questioning my loyalty?" Holly asked indignantly.

"You said it, I didn't," Soozie retorted. With a toss of her hair, she marched away.

Holly just stood there, hands on her hips and her mouth scrunched up in displeasure. Then she gave a wry shrug.

"Take two deep breaths," she counseled Bess. She followed her own advice, exhaling loudly. "There. That's better. Thank heaven for yoga. Breathing puts everything into perspective. Too bad Soozie doesn't practice it," she added. "It might adjust her attitude."

Bess's feeling of well-being was rapidly deflating. "I'm so sorry," she said. "I feel as though I've let you down. I didn't realize I was supposed to bring Casey. I didn't even ask her if she wanted to come with me—"

"No, *I'm* the one who should apologize, for Soozie." Holly returned warmly. "Believe me, if Casey didn't exist, Soozie would have found some other test for you to fail."

Leading Bess toward the buffet table, Holly went on in a low, confiding voice. "Please don't take it personally, Bess. Soozie wants more power around here, and she seems to have decided I'm in her way. I brought you in, so of course she has to try to knock you out. I just want you to know that in-fighting isn't what Kappa's about."

"And it's obviously not about dieting, either!" Bess exclaimed as they arrived in front of a sumptuous spread of goodies. Her eyes widened at the spectacle: little cakes with hard white icing and decorative pink squiggles, individual pear tarts glistening under a golden glaze, fluffy scones.

"If this is how Kappa entertains, Holly, how do you stay so thin? Tell me breathing's the secret, and I'll start yoga tomorrow."

"It's all bean sprouts and springwater except during rush," Holly teased. "Dig in, Bess. But don't take the lemon squares. Soozie made them and they're probably poisoned. Just kidding," she added as she put a lemon square on her own plate and headed off to mingle with some of the other freshman girls.

Normally Bess would have enjoyed sampling the desserts, but she had spent the past two hours making the rounds of Wilder's sororities. She didn't think she could look at another tea sandwich. Besides, her encounter with Soozie killed what little appetite she had left.

If it weren't for Soozie, Kappa would be the perfect place for her. Well, almost perfect. It would only be truly perfect if Nancy and George pledged with her. But she knew that wasn't going to happen.

Nancy and George had made it clear that they didn't want to pledge a sorority. Bess didn't take it personally. She knew that if they spent some time here, they'd agree that Kappa was a great place: no paper dolls and no screaming nonconformists, either; health-conscious but with terrific desserts. Unfortunately, Bess knew that her two best friends wouldn't give it a chance.

That was another reason Bess wanted so desperately to become a Kappa. She'd felt so alone her first few days at Wilder. But if she pledged Kappa, she'd be surrounded by new friends. There'd always be someone to talk to or go to meals with or double date—

A nearby conversation interrupted her thoughts "And then the president said he would only sign the bill if ..."

She wished Nancy and George were there then to overhear the conversation. They'd be impressed that Kappas discussed politics.

"And then Ginger said to the president ..."

With a surge of embarrassment, Bess realized that the conversation was about *The President's Daughter,* not real-life Washington, D.C. Oh, well. At least they were talking about one of the arts, right? The room was full of dancers, sculptors, and writers, as well as girls who shared her love of theater.

Yes, Kappa was definitely the place for her. A niche here would be the only way she could survive freshman year without Nancy and George at her side. It was also the one sure cure for a daily dose of Leslie King.

But what if Soozie kept her out?

Bess was determined not to let that happen.

Soozie Beckerman or no Soozie Beckerman, she just had to become a Kappa!

This assignment is turning out to be a lot of fun, Nancy thought as she popped yet another episode of *The President's Daughter* into the VCR in the lounge. The show was really enjoyable. Settling back to watch Casey do her stuff, Nancy smiled. Even after two hours of solid TV viewing, Nancy knew she was in no danger of becoming a couch potato—especially not on the lounge couch, with its sagging springs. The girls in the suite had nicknamed the couch "the Black Hole." They joked about how many freshmen had been swallowed up by that spineless pile of springy cushions.

Suddenly great sadness welled up inside her. There was an emptiness in the pit of her stomach that had nothing to do with hunger.

Ned, she realized abruptly.

She missed him.

It would have been fun watching these episodes together. Then they'd talk about the show, and Ned would probably give her some ideas for her interview with Casey.

Nancy pictured him the last time she'd seen him, just after they had broken up. The pain in his eyes had been awful to see, and a part of her had longed to say the words that would put the sparkle back in them.

Lying wouldn't have changed anything,

though. And the fact was that she was more eager than ever to try new things. Ned wanted everything, including their relationship, to stay exactly the same.

At least Nancy knew she could count on the support of her father. "One thing is certain about you, Nancy," her father had said just before she left for Wilder University. "Whatever courses you choose, whatever career decision you make, you're not going to be a spectator at life's banquet. You're going to want to taste everything." Carson Drew, a successful lawyer, had always encouraged Nancy in her quest for new experiences. Nancy knew that if her mother had lived past Nancy's childhood, she, too, would have cheered her on.

Even Hannah Gruen, the protective housekeeper who'd help raise Nancy, understood that Nancy needed room to grow. Why couldn't Ned?

One thing was certain, Nancy realized now as she turned her attention from herself to the TV screen. The next love in her life was going to be able to take risks to have fun.

As luck would have it, Peter Goodwin chose that moment to saunter into the lounge. "Nancy!" he exclaimed. "I've been looking for you. Want to have an adventure?"

Stephanie slammed the phone down so hard she almost cracked the plastic receiver. She had never hung up on her father before. They'd never even had a fight.

When her mother was alive, Stephanie was closer to her than to her father. Mr. Keats was a devoted father, but he couldn't spend much time with Stephanie because of his busy law practice. After her mother's death, Stephanie became the center of his life. He took her to fabulous restaurants, to the theater and ballet, and on vacations to Europe and Hawaii. He even took her with him to business and social functions so she could meet his colleagues and clients.

Stephanie loved her father, and she appreciated the way he treated her as an equal, not as a kid. Always—until today.

She couldn't believe he'd just canceled their Christmas ski trip to Switzerland. No, he hadn't canceled it, he was just taking someone else—a new girlfriend. A new *young* girlfriend.

The conversation replayed itself in her mind.

"I know you'll like Kiki," he had said. "You two have a lot in common."

"You mean she's under twenty-one and can't order wine with dinner?" Stephanie tried to make it sound like a joke, but her voice cracked.

"Not exactly. Actually, she's twenty-eight."

Stephanie was so shocked she could hardly breathe, much less speak. Twenty-eight?

Stephanie couldn't remember the rest of the

conversation. Not only was her father embarrassing her by dating someone so young, he was taking Kiki to Switzerland in her place.

Her own father had totally betrayed her.

Of course it was probably Kiki's idea not to invite Stephanie to join them. She was probably hoping that Stephanie would just disappear from their lives now that she was in college.

The door to Stephanie's room burst open, and Casey came in with another box.

"Jeez! I didn't think I had this many shoes!" Casey laughed.

Stephanie watched in furious silence as Casey unpacked her famous collection of sneakers. But Stephanie knew that she wasn't really mad at Casey.

In fact, the more she saw of Casey and her possessions, the harder it was to dislike her. Stephanie wasn't one to make friends—there were so few people on her level who interested her. Casey Fontaine was probably the one freshman at Wilder University who was her equal, though.

Stephanie could just see the two of them skiing the Alps at Christmastime, mopeding around Bermuda during spring break. Of course, it would be only a matter of time before Casey saw the star potential in Stephanie and insisted on introducing her to Hollywood's top producers and agents.

But Stephanie was in such a rotten mood, it felt good to take it out on Casey.

"What size shoe do you wear, Steph?" Casey asked as she put a pair of lace-trimmed, sequin-spattered hightops into one of four hanging shoe bags.

"Eight," Stephanie said grudgingly, feeling as though she were giving away a secret. "And I loathe being called Steph. It sounds like some kind of disease."

Casey didn't seem to take offense. "I'm a seven and a half, but a lot of the European sneakers don't come in half sizes, so I'm loaded with eights." She handed Stephanie an outrageous pair of leopard-spotted somethings that only technically fit the definition of sneakers. They were canvas and laced up, but they boasted two-inch spool heels and open toes.

Stephanie owned one pair of sneakers, which she wore only on the tennis court. She had nothing but contempt for women who wore exercise clothing and footgear for civilian life. It was so tacky. But, Stephanie admitted to herself, the leopard thingies were gorgeous.

"Go for it," Casey encouraged her. "It's amazing, isn't it? The power of a costume to change what you feel on the inside? Those would look fabulous on you, by the way, Stephanie. Borrow them anytime."

Stephanie suddenly felt as though she'd been tricked out of her rotten mood. She was dying to try on the gaudy sneakers, but instead she tossed them onto Casey's bed. "There's something icky about wearing other people's shoes," she said distastefully.

"Hey, I don't have hoof-and-mouth disease!" her new roommate returned. "But suit yourself," she added easily, putting the sneakers into one of the shoe bags in her closet.

"Besides," Stephanie went on, *"I'm* not the borrower in this crowd."

Casey peered at her from beneath flame-colored eyebrows. "Oh, yeah? What's that supposed to mean?"

"If you'd met Kara, you'd know what I mean. I'm surprised Kara bothered to bring anything with her to school at all. She seems to find whatever she needs in other people's rooms."

"Is that why you have that heavy-duty lock on your desk drawer?"

"Your money's safe enough," Stephanie said, avoiding a direct answer to Casey's question. "She's not like Julie, my ex-roommate who stole things and sold them to buy drugs."

Casey acted stunned, as if she didn't know whether or not to believe Stephanie.

"If Kara borrows something from you, you'll get it back—eventually," Stephanie continued. "Along with a hurt, surprised look if you're not grateful at having been so honored."

"I bet you have something nice to say about everyone," Casey prodded.

Stephanie stretched out on her bed. "Well, let's see—our RA, Dawn Steiger, has been especially weepy lately. Her boyfriend, Peter Goodwin, just broke up with her."

"Yeah? That's too bad," Casey said sincerely.

"Mmm, a lot of girls on campus wouldn't agree with you about that. I don't think Peter will be lonely for long."

"Sounds like you'd like to help make sure of that," Casey teased.

Stephanie didn't rise to the bait. She didn't feel like telling Casey about how she had already made a play for Peter and it hadn't led anywhere. Besides, Peter seemed smitten with Nancy Drew. Stephanie couldn't imagine why he preferred the Girl Scout to her, but if he did, he wasn't worth pursuing.

"Not me, thank you," Stephanie said. "Besides, Dawn would probably crawl under a rock and die if one of us in the suite started dating Peter. Don't you just hate those possessive types?" she drawled.

"Well, actually," Casey said, "I'm one myself. Not about my *things*—I'll even lend my car if someone really needs it—but Hollywood kind of cured me of boyfriend-lending. I mean, there nobody's hands-off, not even after you're married. I remember my lawyer once said that in Hollywood marriage is the warm-up for the main act—divorce. It seems like everyone has a boyfriend or girlfriend on the side."

Stephanie felt a sudden prickly sensation behind her eyelids that felt suspiciously like tears trying to happen. Hearing the word *girlfriend* reminded Stephanie of her conversation with her father. For a brief instant, she was almost tempted to tell Casey about her father's new young girlfriend. Instantly she squelched the impulse. What was the point? Nothing Casey might say or do could make the situation any better—and Stephanie couldn't bear to be pitied.

Instead, Stephanie went on dishing the local cast of characters in Suite 301. Casey grinned and nodded as Stephanie's barbs flew through the air.

"Let me see if I've got this straight," the actress said, tucking another empty suitcase under her bed, then stretching out on top of her green silk coverlet. "According to you, Ginny's a walking mass of anxieties, Liz is a know-it-all New Yorker, and Eileen is one of those smiley-face have-a-great-day types who make you want to throw up. Oh, and no one as good-looking as Reva has a right to be so smart about computers. I don't know what your career plans are, Stephanie, but you might just have a great future as a gossip columnist."

Casey propped herself up on one elbow to look at her new roommate. "But you left someone out. What about Nancy? Don't tell me she's the one person around here you actually like."

"Me like Nancy. Are you kidding? I was just saving the worst for last. She's a control freak. Watch out for her, Casey. Especially when she's interviewing you. She's ruthlessly ambitious. Don't believe her for a minute if she says something's off the record—she'll do anything to get a juicy story."

"Well, thanks for the warning," Casey said, her expression neutral. "But what about you, Stephanie? What do I have to watch out for in you?"

Stephanie smiled sweetly. "Everything," she answered. It was the only honest thing she had uttered all day.

# CHAPTER 5

Nancy pressed the Pause button on the VCR remote control. Then she turned to look at Peter.

"An adventure?" she echoed "Sure. I'm ready. Let's go!"

"I like your attitude," Peter said with a grin. "Not to throw cold water on your spontaneity, but what I had in mind is happening *tomorrow* night. It's an improvisational theater group called the Ten O'Clock News, and I thought it might interest you, being a journalist and all."

Nancy's heart gave a hop, skip, and a jump—and not just because Peter was asking her out. She loved the way he'd casually called her a journalist, as if she were already out in the world reporting.

"It sounds great," she said. "I'm really glad you thought of me."

"Well, it's not the first time I've thought of you," Peter said. He began toying with a loose thread hanging from the side of the couch. "So does that mean you're accepting the invitation?"

"Oh, Peter, I'd love to, but—"

The handsome premed student made a wry face. "*But* is the saddest word in the English language. Let me guess, you and Ned are on again." Peter tugged on the thread, and it began to unravel from the couch.

"It's not Ned," Nancy said. "It's Dawn."

Peter looked uncomfortable at the mention of his ex-girlfriend. "Dawn and I are just friends now." Peter stared at the thread growing longer in his hand. Then he looked Nancy straight in the eye. "I think you and I could be more than friends. A lot more."

Peter's directness was like a breath of fresh air after what had become a suffocating relationship with Ned. Nancy felt as if something important was about to happen. Something between her and Peter that might change her life.

"You're not afraid to take chances, are you?" she asked softly.

"You can't be a great doctor if you're afraid to take chances. Or a great journalist," he added.

"Or have much fun," Nancy said.

He broke into a lopsided grin. "Exactly. So what do you think? Am I worth the risk?"

"If I say yes, will you have pity on the poor couch and stop unraveling it?"

He looked down at his fingers. He released the thread. "It's a deal," he said. "Say yes to me, and the couch lives."

"Yes," Nancy said. "But—"

Peter groaned. "There's that word again."

"But I want to talk to Dawn first. I don't want her feelings to get hurt."

Nancy mentally crossed her fingers. She hoped she hadn't turned Peter off by mentioning Dawn again. It wasn't as if she was going to ask her RA's permission to go out with Peter. It was just that Nancy liked Dawn. She didn't want to be part of the hurt that Dawn felt whenever Peter's name was mentioned.

Peter was looking out the window, where oak trees glowed golden in the late afternoon sun. Nancy noticed that the muscles in his neck were taut. She wondered if he was thinking about Dawn, too. Peter ran his fingers through his tousled dark hair and turned to face Nancy. There was an intensity to his dark eyes that Nancy hadn't noticed a moment before.

Peter was different from the other guys she'd met at school, and not only because he was older than the freshmen she was usually surrounded by. There was something else about him besides his maturity that appealed to her. She tried to guess what he was thinking, but he was a mystery to her.

A very attractive mystery.

"Sure," he finally said, turning back to face her. "You're right. Talk to Dawn. I wasn't trying to do anything behind her back. It's just that I feel awkward around her now."

Nancy was impressed with Peter's honesty. Lots of guys wouldn't admit to feeling uncomfortable. "I'm glad you think so, too."

"But what if she says she just can't handle it?" Peter asked. "Then what will you do?"

"I don't know," Nancy said honestly. But one thing she did know—she was going to hold her breath until she had Dawn's answer.

Casey walked into the lounge just as Peter was leaving.

"Oh, I'm sorry, am I interrupting something?" she asked.

"No, it's okay," Nancy said. "Casey, I'd like you to meet Peter Goodwin. He lives on the second floor here in Thayer. Peter, this is Casey—"

"Fontaine, the TV star, I know." Peter said, finishing Nancy's introduction. "I'd recognize you anywhere with that famous red hair, which, by the way, is decidedly shorter than it was on your show." He smiled as they shook hands.

Casey laughed and put her hand to her head.

"Yes, well, this is part of my new life. New hair, new home, new challenges."

"I'd say college will be a challenge all right, but I don't know if it can measure up to the bright lights of Hollywood," Peter replied, then glanced at his watch.

"It was good to meet you, Casey," Peter said. "Sorry I can't stay, but I'm late."

"Me, too. I'm due at rehearsal," Casey said as she started for the door. "Nancy, I just dropped by to find out when you want to do our interview."

"Is tomorrow morning all right?" Nancy asked. She had meant to ask Casey before, but when things got icy between Casey and Stephanie, Nancy decided to wait till a more appropriate time to ask.

"Sure, what time?" Casey asked.

"Nine, if that's not too early for you," Nancy said.

"Are you kidding? I'm so used to early mornings on the set, I wake up confused if it's light outside."

"I'm heading in the same direction as the theater," Peter said.

"Great, we can walk together," Casey said.

Peter's hand brushed Nancy's shoulder. "I'll pick you up tomorrow night at seven, Nancy. We can grab a bite to eat before the show."

"Sounds good," Nancy said as Peter and Casey headed out the door of the suite.

Sounds great! She said to herself, still feeling the warmth of his touch on her arm.

I think I'm in love, Will said to himself. How else to explain why it was so much fun to watch a girl rearrange the bulletin board at Java Joe's?

But, really, she made an art form of it. And she was so considerate. Unlike some people, she didn't obliterate other announcements and messages with hers. She carefully pulled out pushpins and thumbtacks, moved pieces of paper closer together as if she were designing a mosaic. Magically she created an empty space right in the middle for the Earthworks poster.

"Well done," he said. "Your best yet. I'd say it deserves a kiss. Plus a cappuccino. In that order."

"Two kisses," George said teasingly.

"You're a tough negotiator," Will said as he bent to deliver the promised kisses.

When their kips met, Will felt an electric current surge through his body. It happened every time they kissed, but instead of becoming familiar, the intensity grew and grew.

Will knew that he was in love with George, and that she was experiencing the same emotions about him. He didn't want to rush things, but it felt so right being with her.

Behind them he could hear the sounds of

coffee beans being ground, people laughing, and someone shouting, "Oh, no!" as a cup clattered to the floor and broke. But the racket wasn't loud enough to drown out the sound of his own heartbeat.

He would ask her soon.

Bess glanced nervously at her wristwatch. She was due at rehearsal in fifteen minutes, and the theater was a five-minute walk from Kappa.

Bess had been searching the downstairs rooms for Holly to say goodbye and thanks, but the Kappa vice president had disappeared.

Fortunately Eileen O'Connor's friendly face materialized out of the throng. Eileen seemed as serious about rushing Kappa as Bess was. They had already met several times because Eileen was one of Nancy's suitemates. But now they were developing a relationship on their own, independent of Nancy and the rest of the Thayer 301 crowd.

"Bess! I've been trying to say hello to you ever since you walked in, but you kept getting whisked away. Terrific place, isn't it?"

"I love it!" Bess said. "Don't you think Nancy would, too?" she added wistfully. Her eyes scanned the details of the room, from the unmatched but harmonious silk-covered chairs to the moldings that the Kappas had stripped and refinished with their own hands.

"She'd take one look and say it's a great place to visit but she wouldn't want to live here," Eileen countered with a little laugh. "Face it, Bess. The *Wilder Times* is Nancy's new home away from home. Speaking of which, Nancy's interview subject for the paper just moved into our suite."

Bess was stunned. "Casey?" She wondered why Nancy hadn't mentioned it, then realized she hadn't even seen Nancy in a couple of days. They were drifting farther and farther apart, she thought with a pang of sadness.

Sometimes Bess wished that she and Nancy and George had gone to different schools after all. Then she wouldn't expect them to be as close as they had always been in the past. But with the three of them at Wilder, the illusion of togetherness was sometimes too painful for her to bear.

Except that if she'd gone somewhere else, there wouldn't be a sorority like Kappa, and she wouldn't be in *Grease!* . . . oops! "Thou shalt not be late" was one of the iron rules of theater, as her friend Brian Daglian kept telling her, and she was in danger of being the late Bess Marvin yet again.

"I've *got* to get to rehearsal," she said to Eileen. "Holly's disappeared—she must be giving another guided tour upstairs. Could you say goodbye and thanks for me? And tell her I had a great time? And gained about ten pounds?" Her anxieties about Soozie had finally been no match for those gorgeous pastries.

"I'll be glad—" Eileen began, then broke off when she realized Bess wasn't paying attention to her. "Bess? Hello?"

"Listen," Bess whispered, nodding toward two girls standing nearby. They were talking about Kappa.

"It's so hopelessly square. I mean, what's with the no-smoking policy?" griped one of them. "Is this a sorority or a hospital waiting room? I say let's go for an invite to pledge Theta. At least they know how to have fun."

"Absolutely," agreed the other, a rail-thin blond. "Dave says you can smoke anything you like there."

"He should know. He's the man. Let's go over to his frat, Zeta, and see what he's holding," the dark-haired girl said. "I could use an upper after all this snoozy chitchat."

"It's a good thing I get a generous clothing allowance. If my parents knew I was buying designer drugs instead of designer jeans . . ."

As the two girls moved out of earshot, Bess and Eileen stared at each other.

"Heavy-duty," Eileen whispered. "Makes me think of poor Julie. I wonder if this Dave was her connection. Sounds like he's the local drug king."

Dave . . . Zeta . . .

A shudder ran through Bess. Could it be that the campus drug king was the same Dave who'd come terrifyingly close to date-raping her at the Zeta frat party? It made chilling sense.

"If Julie had turned her dealer in," Eileen said, "maybe there would be fewer drugs on campus."

But Julie had refused to name the person who sold her drugs. Suppose it was Dave. Maybe, Bess thought, if she went to see Julie in person, she could convince her to talk to campus security. They could go together and report Dave.

Bess had no proof one way or the other that Dave was "the man." Just a head full of suspicions.

If Bess didn't have a rehearsal, she'd follow those two girls. Because if their Dave was Dave Cantera, she might have a way to get even with him, and get him off campus and out of her dreams forever.

If only Julie would talk . . .

The man in the shadows of a building on the Wilder campus was about to give up. He had been waiting hours to catch a glimpse of his beloved.

Finally there she was—as beautiful as ever. She reminded him of an angel. He imagined an aura of gold encircling her head, infusing the red of her hair with a fiery brightness.

Wait, who was that with her?

Her cardboard Hollywood boyfriend?

No, it couldn't be. Not here.

No, just looks a little like him. The same superficially handsome type.

He had the kind of looks girls always liked. Didn't they know that men like him were shallow and fickle love-'em-and-leave-'em types?

How could she be so foolish to fall for guys like that again and again? He balled his hands into tight fists thinking about the men he had seen Casey with in the past.

Now this one was making her laugh, damn him. She was throwing her head back and roaring, the way she always did on the show.

He's probably just waiting for his chance to make a move on her. Doesn't she know the chance she's taking?

I'll follow them, then. To watch her, to protect her, to take her . . .


Peter was feeling good as he left Thayer with Casey. Casey seemed nice, not stuck-up the way he'd expected a TV star to be. He knew a lot of guys would be turned on by her looks and her fame. But she didn't have that effect on him. At least not after he'd met Nancy.

"So, you and Nancy are going out tomorrow night?" Casey asked.

Peter blushed. He nodded, trying to conceal the rush of embarrassment he felt. For some reason just the thought of dating Nancy made him feel like a little kid with a hopeless crush. Was the possibility of a relationship with Nancy really that hopeless?

"I just met her today, but I can tell already that she's a really great person. I'm glad she's in my suite," Casey continued, easily making conversation. "Have you two been dating long?"

Peter began to feel a little more at ease. There was no reason not to talk to Casey about Nancy. "Actually, tomorrow will be our first date." Peter felt himself blushing again and fought to control the blood rushing to his face.

Casey didn't seem surprised by his remark. "Well, you two look really good together. I hope it works out," Casey said.

So do I, Peter silently agreed. He realized he had started to whistle as he thought about his date with Nancy. That is, if Dawn didn't spoil it by sending Nancy on some kind of guilt trip. No, Dawn wouldn't do that. No matter how devastated she was by their breakup, she wouldn't intentionally sabotage his life.

He wished he hadn't let things go as far as they had with Dawn. It was too late now to do anything about that. It was too late for lots of things.

Without realizing it, Peter was already at the science building. "Well, here's where I head off," Peter said to Casey. "I promised one of my friends that I'd help him unravel the mysteries of microbiology."

"The very word *microbiology* makes my head spin," Casey said. "Thank heaven for Geology 101—Rocks for Jocks. Otherwise I'd probably celebrate my fiftieth birthday before I fulfilled my freshman science requirement."

Suddenly a voice called out, "Casey!"

The actress turned around, then waved vigorously at the pretty blond-haired girl hurrying their way. "Hi, Bess. On your way to rehearsal? Yikes, we're almost late! Where did the time go?" she asked with a glance at her watch. "And me the pro. We'd better scoot."

"See you," Casey called to Peter as she and Bess hustled toward the theater.

As Peter turned up the walkway to the science building, she noticed a couple passing by, holding hands and looking as if they didn't have a care in the world. If only his life could be that carefree.

He watched the couple stop and kiss goodbye.

He thought about kissing Nancy the way he had that night at the lake. It was impulsive and it was over much too soon.

He and Nancy . . .

Peter realized right then that he was falling in love with Nancy Drew.

# CHAPTER 6

Nancy paced around the room she shared with Kara. She couldn't sit still, but she didn't want to do what she knew had to be done, either. She rearranged the photographs on her dresser top, sharpened a couple of pencils, then considered reorganizing her bookshelves.

Anything to put off the moment when she knocked on Dawn's door. Perhaps if she alphabetized her books by author instead of just dividing them up by subject . . .

"Hey, Nancy?" Kara looked up from her desk, pushing back her long brown hair.

Nancy stopped and offered her roommate an apologetic smile. "Sorry, Kara. I know I must be annoying—"

"No, you're not bugging me," she interrupted. "It's this sonnet I'm trying to write.

I'm stuck and"—Kara's face lit up—"wait a minute, you inspired me." Kara bent over her paper and scribbled several lines. " 'When I grow faint with longing for your face / I get up from my bed and start to pace.' That's it! Thanks, Nancy!" She frowned for a moment, then went on. "I think I'd better change *bed* to *chair*. It keeps the rhythm and won't get as many snickers if we have to read these aloud."

"You certainly have the iambic pentameter down," Nancy said.

Kara's pen flew over the paper. She read aloud as she wrote: " 'And in my nervous circling of the floor / Your face invades my vision all the more.' "

"Kara! That's great!" Nancy exclaimed. "Is it about Vic?"

Vic was Kara's ex-boyfriend. He'd broken up with her right before Nancy exposed his role in a school betting scandal.

Kara nodded sadly. "I still miss him. And the really hard part is that he was—you know—my first. The one I'm going to have to remember all my life."

The way I'm going to remember Ned, Nancy thought sadly. Because even though we never slept together, he was my first real love.

And the way Dawn was going to remember Peter.

Kara turned her attention back to the paper in front of her. " 'I ran against the wind and lost the race / But even if I could, I'd not erase / The memories that I am doomed to store / Until I stand, at last, at heaven's door.' " She looked up at Nancy, the familiar self-confident grin back in place.

"Hey, that's good, isn't it?" Kara said as she put her pen back to the paper. "I never expected Vic to help me get an A in Freshman Comp."

"I guess that's what makes college so much fun," Nancy said. "The unexpected."

Kara nodded, but her mind was back on her poem.

The unexpected . . . Like falling in love with Peter Goodwin, Nancy thought as she summoned her courage and headed for Dawn's room.

The wind picked up as Bess and Casey hurried toward the theater. The sun was just setting, and the quad was filled with students relaxing after another week of school.

Bess smiled at Casey. "I hear you just moved into Nancy Drew's suite," she said.

"Good old Thayer 301," Casey returned with a laugh. "What a collection of characters! I'm not sure about some of them—like my roommate for instance—but Nancy's great."

"I told you," Bess said, pleased that Casey and Nancy had hit it off.

A passing student did a double-take as he recognized Casey. "Hi, Ginger," he called out.

"Hi, there!" Casey replied cheerfully. "Dork," she added under her breath, so only Bess could hear.

"That must get pretty old, being called Ginger, I mean."

"Yeah," Casey admitted. "But I should be used to it by now. It happens all the time. I guess after watching *PD* for years, people think Ginger is real."

"Speaking of which," Bess said, "are those TV kisses with Charley for real?" she blurted out. Instantly she regretted the question. It was just the sort of dopey thing a starstruck fan would ask.

Casey didn't seem to mind. "Most of them are real. It took us about thirty seconds to fall in love. Of course, sometimes we hated each other, and we had to fake it. Do you remember the stalker episode?"

"Who could forget it?" Bess asked. "I saw the first part again last night, and it was as scary as the first time."

"Well, Charley and I weren't even speaking during the shooting. He'd asked me to move in with him, and I'd said I wasn't ready, and he went ballistic. Then we had to make this episode in which he saved my life and we were all over each other."

Bess was thrilled that Casey was being so open with her.

"That episode was almost enough to cure me of acting all together," Casey went on. "And the worst part was that this stupid tabloid reporter kept following me around, like he was spying on me—which I guess he was in a way. It would have been scary if he hadn't been such a klutz. He was always dropping his tape recorder or tripping over the curb to get to me. Actually, it would have been funny if it had been part of a *PD* episode, but in real life it was very annoying. Just in case you were thinking my old life was sheer glamour."

"Ugh," Bess said. "Couldn't you do anything about it?"

"There's not much you can do. I mean even reporters have rights. Freedom of the press and all that. He didn't actually do anything to me."

"You must be glad to be halfway across the country from him," Bess remarked.

Casey didn't say anything. She wished she could confide her real fears to Bess, about the phone calls and the letters, but it was too risky. Besides, they were at the theater and Casey wasn't about to have that conversation within hearing distance of the entire cast of *Grease!*

No, she had to keep that secret to herself, at least for now.

\* \* \*

Nancy stood in front of Dawn's closed door. The RA had the only single in the suite—it was just off the lounge. As she knocked, Nancy felt as uncomfortable as she could ever remember feeling.

It didn't help that Dawn greeted her with a welcoming grin. Nancy would have been happy to see her, too, if she didn't feel so awkward about the conversation she was about to initiate.

"Can I come in?" Nancy asked. "I wanted to talk to you about something."

"Sure," Dawn said. "That's why I'm here."

Dawn waved Nancy onto her bed and sat down at her desk. "So, what's up?"

Nancy glanced around the room. If I had a single it would probably look a lot like this, she said to herself.

Books . . . a huge lighted globe . . . a framed print of Josef Albers's yellow squares, simple and powerful, that Nancy recognized from the Art Institute in Chicago. The bed was neat but cozy, with a knitted off-white spread that had to have come from Ireland. The throw pillows were all in the same neutral color, but no two had been knitted in the same pattern, so the effect was anything but boring.

Dawn misunderstood Nancy's silence. "Is it about Ned?" she prompted.

"Sort of," Nancy said. "Actually, I think I've

met someone who might help me get over Ned, and he seems to want to."

"That's great!" Dawn said enthusiastically. "Who is he? What's his name?"

Nancy forced herself to look the other girl in the eye. She took a deep breath. "Peter Goodwin."

"Peter?" Dawn echoed.

"We have a date for Saturday night," Nancy said. "I—we—wanted to be upfront about it."

"Oh," Dawn said.

Nancy saw the hurt in the RA's eyes, and she felt terrible for causing her new pain.

There was an awkward silence. Nancy wished she knew what to say to make Dawn feel better. She tried to imagine herself in Dawn's place. How would she feel if a girl she knew told her she was dating Ned? Nancy felt a twinge just thinking about it.

After a long moment Dawn regained her composure. "Okay, well, you've told me. Now I'd better get back to what I was doing." Dawn stood and walked toward the door, making it obvious that she wanted Nancy to go.

Nancy hesitated. She didn't want to leave things with Dawn this way. "But, Dawn, can't we talk about this?" She wanted to be friends with Dawn. They had so much in common, Nancy thought wryly as she started for the door. Especially their taste in men.

"See you later, Nancy," Dawn said dismissively. She was holding the door open.

Nancy walked out into the lounge. The door clicked shut behind her. Then she heard the bed springs creak, followed by a loud silence.

Bess was ready to burst into tears. The way Brian was scolding her for being late, you'd have thought it was opening night of *Grease!* and she'd delayed the entire production.

"You have to be *professional,*" he said, for what seemed like the hundredth time.

The scene they were in together wasn't even scheduled to be rehearsed for another half hour, and still he was carrying on.

He and Bess were sitting in the back row of the theater. The two juniors who had the leads were dancing superbly up on the stage, but Brian seemed more interested in making Bess feel miserable than in watching them.

"And what's with your eyelids?" he continued in the same muted but harsh tones. "They're all swollen. Maybe you should wear dark glasses or something."

Bess whipped out her compact and looked into the mirror. "Oh, no," she moaned, forgetting to whisper—which of course earned another stern glance from Brian. "It must be a reaction to the cucumber slices!"

"The what?"

"Oh, never mind." Bess felt her stomach

clench. Had she looked like this at all those sorority parties? With a rush of relief, she remembered that she'd used the washroom at Kappa toward the end of the party, and she'd checked herself out in the mirror. Eyelids the size of marshmallows would not have escaped her attention.

But that didn't change one important fact. Brian was supposed to be her friend. And here he was treating her horribly!

Bess expected behavior like that from her roommate and Soozie Beckerman, but not Brian.

"You can't show up for rehearsal like that, Bess. You look terrible," he said.

That was the last straw. Bess got up and ran out of the auditorium. Giving way to full-blown sobs, she didn't hear Brian come up behind her. She jumped when he put his arms around her in a bear hug, then she recognized the lime scent of his aftershave, and she turned to sob into his shoulder.

"Bess, I'm so sorry," he crooned. "I'm a nervous wreck, and I took it out on you. Forgive me?"

"Oh, Brian," she wailed, "why didn't anyone tell me that freshman year would be so complicated? I just don't know if I can take all the ups and downs. I mean, I'm just not used to people hating me, and—"

"Shh. I don't hate you. You know that." He

awkwardly patted her hair. "Please forgive me?"

"I guess so," she said quietly. "I forgive you. And now I think I'd better go throw some cold water on my face. Because the show must go on, right?"

"That's the Bess Marvin I know and love," Brian said. "I'll wait for you. Then we can go back in together."

When she emerged five minutes later, he nodded his blond head approvingly. "Good as new. Come backstage with me," he went on, holding out his hand. "I want you to meet a friend of mine."

He led her past the brightly lit makeup room, into a maze of rooms that Bess had never seen before.

"Where are we?" she asked.

"That's where the sets get built," Brian said, "and here's the lighting workshop. Yo, Chris," he called out softly, attracting the attention of an intense-looking guy who was holding up colored gels and frowning at them.

"Hi, Bri."

"I want you to meet Bess Marvin. Bess, this is Chris Vogel. He just joined the crew. Be nice to him, or he'll put a green spot on you."

She held out her hand. "Hi, Chris, glad to meet you."

"Brian told me a lot about you," Chris said.

"He says you're very gung ho about theater. Sorry you didn't make it into Drama 101."

"Well, at least I made it into *Grease!*" Bess said. "Speaking of which—" She turned to Brian.

"Right," he said. "We'd better get back to the auditorium. But I really wanted you two to meet."

"I'm glad we did," Bess said enthusiastically. "See you later, Chris."

As she and Brian hurried back through the maze, she playfully nudged her friend. "Chris Vogel from your drama class? Isn't he The One?"

Brian turned bright red. "So what do you think?"

"I think he's really nice," Bess said. "And I think you two look great together."

Brian sighed happily. "And next I'm going to find someone for you, Bess. I haven't forgotten my promise."

Bess was sure he meant to keep his word. But was there really a guy for her on the Wilder campus? If so, where was he hiding? And when would she meet him. *When?*

# CHAPTER 7

Kara rummaged through her drawers. "I thought I had a light blue sweater that matched this skirt," she said. "I remember I wore it last week."

"Actually, that was my sweater," Nancy reminded her roommate.

"Oh, yeah, right, I forgot," Kara said, looking up from her dresser at Nancy. "You have so many nice clothes."

Nancy could read the look in her roommate's eyes. "Would you like to borrow it again?" she asked.

"No, I just remembered, I wore that sweater to the Pi Phi party last weekend. I really should wear something different—like maybe your peach sweater."

Nancy cringed. She had worn that sweater

only twice herself. It was new and one of her favorites. She had been planning to wear it on her date with Peter. But before she could protest, Kara had already taken the sweater from Nancy's drawer and pulled it over her head.

"Perfect," Kara said, admiring her reflection in the full-length mirror. "I'm getting good vibes from the girls at Pi Phi. I think they're going to invite me to pledge."

"That's great," Nancy said with some enthusiasm. *Maybe then she'll raid her sorority sisters' closets instead of mine,* she thought.

"Gotta run. 'Bye," Kara called to Nancy as she raced out the door.

" 'Bye," Nancy said. She heard the door to the suite slam shut and breathed a sigh of relief. Nancy knew she could have done worse for a roommate, but sometimes she wished she had a single. Sometimes it was hard to hear herself think with Kara in the room. And Nancy had a lot to think about—like her talk with Dawn. . . .

Nancy stood in front of the mirror and pulled a brush through her reddish blond hair. Her talk with Dawn hadn't exactly been a success, but then what had she expected? That Dawn would be thrilled that Nancy was dating her ex-boyfriend? Her ex-boyfriend with whom she was still in love?

Nancy could hear a few voices as the last of her suitemates got ready for Friday night parties and dates. She glanced at the stack of *The President's Daughter* videotapes on her desk. She'd made some notes while she was watching and she also had about a page and a half of notes from the magazine articles. Maybe she should review them before her interview with Casey tomorrow morning. She wanted to be prepared.

It was Friday night, though, and Nancy was restless. She didn't feel like working. She wanted to have some fun!

She picked up the phone and dialed George's number. The machine picked up.

"This is George—"

"And this is Pam—"

"We're not in—"

"So please leave a message!"

Nancy waited for the beep, then said, "Hi, George. This is Nancy. I was wondering what you were up to tonight. Give me a call." She hung up and dialed Bess's number. Leslie picked up on the first ring.

"Hi, Leslie. This is Nancy Drew. Is Bess there?"

"No." Leslie never sounded particularly friendly, but now her tone seemed downright hostile.

"Oh, uh, well, do you know where she is or when she'll be back?" Nancy persisted. Maybe she and Bess could go to the Underground together and listen to some music.

"How should I know?" Leslie said in a snotty tone of voice. "I'm not her social secretary. Now, if you don't mind, I was in the middle of a complex equation."

Nancy heard a click and realized that Leslie had hung up. She probably wouldn't bother to tell Bess she'd called even if Bess did get back in time to go out.

Nancy sighed. Well, college was about meeting new people. Maybe she'd meet someone new at the Underground, a dingy, unspectacular cafeteria by day that was transformed at night into an atmospheric hangout for the university's art crowd.

Again Nancy considered going to the office of the *Wilder Times* to work on her article, but the thought of running into Gail there and being given more mindless blurbs to write quickly dispelled that idea. No, tonight was for relaxation.

Nancy pulled on a green cotton sweater, touched up her makeup, and headed out. The lounge was empty. Everyone must have already left, Nancy thought as she stepped around the low coffee table.

A few minutes later Nancy was crossing to the back of Thayer when she heard a strange sound. She stopped to listen. It sounded like something was rummaging in the open Dumpster. A raccoon? Then there was a loud bang as the top of the Dumpster crashed shut.

"Help! Get me out of here!"

It wasn't an animal, Nancy realized. Some-one was trapped inside!

Nancy rushed to the Dumpster and pried open the lid. A man, visibly shaken, climbed out.

"Are you all right?" Nancy asked. She was concerned, but she didn't want to get too close to him. Not only did he smell of garbage, he might be dangerous.

The man nodded and brushed himself off. Nancy noticed he was clutching some crumpled-up papers in one hand. He noticed Nancy star-ing at the papers and stuffed them in his pocket. "Actually, maybe you could help me. I'm looking for a freshman who lives in this dorm. Her name is Casey Fontaine. Do you know her?"

Nancy hesitated. Should she tell the man she was one of Casey's suitemates? Should she be talking to him at all?

Nancy knew she was in a vulnerable situa-tion. It was dark, and there was no one around. Still, she was curious.

"First, why don't you tell me who you are and why you were Dumpster diving behind my dorm," Nancy said.

"My name is Gavin Michaels. I'm a reporter, and I'm doing a story on Casey Fontaine for the *Hollywood Star.*" The man held out his hand, then realized it was covered with dirt from the Dumpster. He wiped it against the seat of his pants and stuffed both hands deep inside his pockets. "Perhaps you could tell me something about her," he prompted.

"I don't think so," Nancy said. This guy is weird, Nancy thought as she walked away. And he had obviously been looking through the Dumpster to find Casey's garbage.

Nancy decided to run back to her room and call campus security before heading to the Underground.

Bess yawned as she and Casey staggered out of the theater. "I feel as though I've lived ten lives today," she said.

"It was a long rehearsal. But it's going to pay off. This production is looking really good already."

"I still think you should have auditioned for one of the leads. Your talent's wasted in such a small role," Bess declared.

"I'm happy just to be onstage," Casey said. "But wait until they do Shakespeare. Then I'll go for the juicy parts."

The wind gusted and leaves swirled around their feet, crunching underfoot. Bess noticed Casey peek back over her shoulder, and did the same. There was no one on the path behind them.

Casey shrugged. "I thought I heard something," she said, sounding a little embarrassed. "I'm probably just being paranoid."

"Maybe it was the wind," Bess said. They listened to the wind and the leaves rustling. All of a sudden Bess did feel spooked. There weren't any people in sight, and the path they were on was poorly lit. She picked up the pace a little. Soon she and Casey were practically jogging.

"Do you think someone's following us?" Bess asked.

"I thought I heard footsteps," Casey answered. "Let's go to my dorm, it's closer."

Soon the girls were in Thayer's lobby, safely behind the double glass doors that were kept locked at night. Bess was huffing and puffing. She wasn't used to getting much exercise, and the running had winded her.

"We should call campus security," Bess said.

"No," Casey replied. "I don't want to make a big deal out of this."

Bess thought a moment. "Then let's see if Nancy is in her room," she suggested.

"I don't know," Casey hesitated.

But Bess insisted. "Come on, Casey. We have to tell someone. Nancy's one of my best friends, and she's really helpful with stuff like this. She'll know what to do."

"Okay," Casey agreed reluctantly. "Let's go find Nancy."

Nancy unlocked her room door and went inside. She locked the door behind her and turned on the light. That's when she looked down at the floor and saw the folded piece of paper with her name on it.

She picked it up and read it.

Dear Nancy,

I'm writing you a note and slipping it under your door because I can't face you quite yet.

I guess it shouldn't have come as a surprise to me that you and Peter would hit it off. Logically maybe I should feel better about Peter going out with someone I like, someone I think is sort of like me. But I guess one of the life lessons I've learned recently is that the heart isn't logical. Mine isn't, anyway.

But even though Peter and I broke up, I still feel a lot for him and it's difficult for me to think of us as totally finished.

But after you left, I took a long, hard look in the mirror and realized the problem is mine, not yours.

I can't say I'm happy about your dating Peter, but I'll handle it. And I won't let it interfere with our relationship. I do want to be your friend as well as your RA.

It took guts for you to come to my room and tell me about Peter, and I want to apologize for reacting so badly.

Sincerely,
Dawn

Nancy folded the letter back up and put it in her desk drawer. Maybe she and Dawn could still be friends. She hoped so.

Nancy had just picked up her phone to call campus security when there was a knock on the door.

"Nancy, are you in there?" she heard Bess ask. The knob turned, but the door was locked.

"Just a minute." Nancy jumped up and unlocked the door. Bess rushed in, followed by Casey. They both seemed to be upset.

"What's wrong?" Nancy asked, concerned.

"Someone was following us, so we ran all the way here from the theater," Bess said. Nancy noticed Bess was flushed.

"We're not *sure* someone followed us," corrected Casey.

"You said you heard footsteps," Bess reminded Casey. "And I got this tingly sensation like I was being watched."

"It could have been another college student on the way home," Casey said reasonably. "I mean, there's no sense in jumping to conclusions."

Nancy thought of Gavin Michaels. He was on campus looking for Casey. It could have been him. "Maybe you *were* being followed," Nancy began.

"I knew you'd believe us," Bess said. "Casey was afraid you'd just think she was being paranoid."

Nancy decided to be direct with Casey. "Do you know someone named Gavin Michaels?" she asked.

Casey's face fell at the mention of the reporter's name.

"You mean *the* Gavin Michaels, who writes for the *Hollywood Star*?" asked Bess.

Both Nancy and Casey turned to look at Bess with disbelief.

"How do *you* know Gavin?" Casey asked.

"Well, I don't exactly know him. I've just read some of his articles," Bess said.

"You *buy* the *Star*?" Casey seemed shocked.

"I don't *buy* it. I just read it when I'm in line at the supermarket," Bess said a little defensively. "He's written a lot about you, hasn't he? I remember one article about you growing up in Springdale. About your dog, Biff. And how you cried when he got hit by a truck. That was so sad."

"My dog's name was Mini, and she died of old age," Casey said.

"What about the article he wrote about the first time you went skiing and ended up on the double black diamond trail?" Bess asked.

"That one was actually true. And I never found out how he knew that." Casey seemed lost in thought for a moment, then she turned to Nancy. "Why do you want to know about him?"

"I just met him—rescued him actually," Nancy replied. "He was stuck in a Dumpster."

"I wish you'd left him there," Casey said. "That's where he and all his stories belong—in the trash."

"Why don't you tell us about him," Nancy said gently.

Casey flopped down on Kara's bed. "There's not a lot to tell. He's one of the sleaziest so-called reporters in Hollywood. He followed me around when I was working on *PD*, but he wasn't allowed to interview me so he talked to everyone and anyone I'd ever met trying to get some dirt on me so he could write some lurid headline that would sell more papers."

"He sounds awful," Bess said.

"He was," Casey agreed. "And the worst part was that even though his stories about me were full of lies, there was always some bit of truth in them. And some of the things he wrote about—like my first time skiing—there's no way he could have known. And other stuff, too. Really personal things—things to do with me and an old boyfriend I had when I was a freshman in high school." Casey blushed.

Nancy thought this Gavin Michaels sounded like a jerk. It also sounded as if he had been harassing Casey in Hollywood. Now he was at Wilder, probably intent on doing the same thing. It was reporters like Gavin Michaels who gave the press a bad name.

"I was about to call campus security when you came," Nancy said, picking up the phone. "Maybe they can do something—"

"No!" Casey interrupted. "You can't call security!"

"Why not?" Nancy was puzzled by Casey's reaction.

"Because campus security might notify my parents, and if they find out, they'll hire body-guards and probably make me move off-campus," Casey said in a rush. "Then I can kiss any hopes of a normal college life goodbye. Besides, it's not like Gavin is a threat. He's just incredibly annoying, like the phone calls and letters—"

"What phone calls? What letters?" Nancy asked. "Has he been harassing you here at Wilder?"

"Promise you won't tell security?" Casey looked Nancy in the eye.

Nancy nodded, and Casey continued. "It's something I haven't told anyone, not even my first roommate. I probably would have scared her half to death." Casey hesitated, then the words came rushing out.

"The phone calls started when I got to Wilder. I don't know who it is—or even if it's a man or a woman. Whoever it is hangs up without speaking."

"And the letters?" Nancy prompted.

"The letters started coming when I was still

in Hollywood. At first I thought they were from an overzealous fan. A lot of boys fall in love with Ginger and don't realize that I'm not like her. They think they know me because they watch the show. But what was weird about the letters was that they included stuff about me that wasn't ever published in any magazine—stuff no one except my family and close friends know about."

"Did you save the letters?" Nancy asked hopefully. Nancy had already decided she'd try to help Casey. Maybe there'd be some clue that would link the letters to Gavin Michaels.

Casey nodded. "They're in a box I haven't unpacked yet. I'll bring them tomorrow morning for our interview." Casey yawned. "I don't know about you two," she said, "but I'm beat. I'm going to bed."

Nancy and Bess said good night to Casey as she left Nancy's room.

"So what do you think?" asked Bess. "Is Gavin Michaels the one making the phone calls and writing the letters?"

Nancy shrugged. "He might be calling Casey's room to see if she's there so he can follow her."

Bess walked over to Nancy's window and looked out. Nancy could tell her friend was nervous about walking back to her dorm alone. "Come on, I'll drive you to Jamison," she suggested.

"Thanks, Nancy," Bess said, obviously relieved. "You're a real lifesaver."

Nancy smiled, but she couldn't stop thinking about Casey. Was the *Hollywood Star* reporter just an unscrupulous journalist, or was he the one obsessed with Casey, writing her love letters and making crank calls?

Or was it just a lovestruck fan, as Casey thought?

Casey didn't seem too worried about Gavin Michaels or the letters or the hang-up phone calls.

Nancy hoped Casey was right not to worry and that her own instincts were wrong. Because her own instincts told her that Casey could be in danger.

# CHAPTER 8

I think you picked a very good morning to suggest indoor swimming," George said to Will as they headed into the shiny new sports complex.

"I can't believe you haven't tried it yet!" Will exclaimed.

"Give me a break! Between crew, running, going to classes, saving the environment, and *you,* I feel as though every moment's taken, and then some," George said, grinning.

As they went through the set of swinging doors, the distinctive smell of chlorine greeted George's nose. Will pushed open another door, and they were greeted by warm, still air. Reflecting the brilliant blue paint, the water in the Olympic-size pool lapped slowly against the concrete walls. No one else was around at this early morning hour.

"To the locker rooms!" George cried. "I can't believe we have the place to ourselves. Let's hurry."

"Back in two minutes," Will said, racing to the men's changing area.

A few minutes later they were both in the water, kicking and splashing. George turned and did a lap of breaststroke as Will executed some dives. When they arrived simultaneously at the shallow end, Will reached across the yellow divider to kiss her softly.

"Even with all that chlorine, you taste sweet," he said. "Say, under the laws of Political Correctness, am I allowed to tell you that you look very sexy in a swimsuit? You're beautiful, George."

"In this old thing? It's just a black tank suit. Hardly what I'd call sexy," she said, suddenly feeling very shy. "But thanks for a lovely compliment, and by the way, you don't look so bad yourself." George dived under the water, unable to trust what might happen next if she stayed near his gorgeous body.

An hour later George and Will walked out of the shiny new sports complex hand in hand.

"I'm glad we got some exercise in early. It doesn't look like a good day to run," George said glancing up at the gray morning sky. The rain that had been threatening since the night before seemed imminent.

"More like mudslide weather," Will agreed.

"Laundry weather for me," George said. "I've got a date with a washer and dryer at the Laundromat."

"I'll go with you," Will suggested. "We can watch our clothes spin dry together."

"I don't know," George teased. "I'm not sure our relationship can stand the test of dirty laundry."

Will put an arm around her waist and pulled her next to him. "Try me," he said as his lips brushed hers.

George felt a shiver of excitement move up her spine. She knew that even her compost heap of a laundry basket wouldn't drive Will away. She imagined what the next few years with Will would be like. They would get to know each other's friends. They would read each other's favorite books and share their jokes and their dreams.

"So what else are you planning to do this weekend, besides laundry?" Will asked.

"Actually, I thought I'd call Nancy and Bess and see what they're up to. I haven't spoken to either of them in a while. Maybe we can all do something together," she said. "Bess loves to go out for Sunday brunch."

"So do I," Will said. "But I like breakfast in bed even better." George was suddenly aware of his closeness, which was delicious but scary, too.

It was time to stop, and she said so.

Will drew a deep breath and ruffled her hair. "Whatever you say. Breakfast time?"

"Terrific." She was suddenly very hungry. "But I think we'd better go to a public place. How about Java Joe's?"

"Fine with me," Will said. "I like the kisses there."

Squinting in the early morning light, the man looked up at the third floor of Thayer Hall, trying to pick out which of the windows belonged to his beloved Casey.

Casey, Casey, Casey.

I didn't mean to scare you last night. I just wanted to be near you.

But you and your blond friend took off like startled rabbits.

I wanted to call out to you to stop, to say that I wasn't a mugger. I would never hurt you, my darling Casey.

I can't bear this separation much longer.

I'm almost done putting the finishing touches on our new home. I know you'll love it.

If you love it only half as much as I love you, we will be blissfully happy there.

I wanted to take you there last night. You looked so beautiful in the moonlight. The twinkling stars in the sky are like fireflies compared to the sparks that fly from your beautiful eyes.

But your blond friend probably wouldn't have understood our need to be alone, totally alone.

So few people understand true love. The need to be with someone. A need stronger than hunger or thirst.

But you can't be surrounded by people all the time.

I'll try to be patient, my love.

Till I find you alone.

Till we can be together, forever.


"Julie, you look fantastic," Bess said sincerely.

Bess was following through on her decision to try to talk Julie Hammerman into telling campus authorities about Dave.

She had borrowed Nancy's car early Saturday morning to visit Julie, who was at the Greenview Clinic recovering from her drug problem.

Julie had put on a much-needed few pounds, and her cheeks, which had always been frighteningly pale, now looked as though blood flowed through them again.

"I don't know about fantastic," Julie returned, "but I'm on my way. I just had some good news, actually. I've been accepted at my mom's old college, in Massachusetts. As soon as I graduate from here, I head east."

"Congratulations!" Bess said. "But I bet they won't have a bakery as good as Spinelli's."

She handed over a box of Italian cookies. They'd looked prettier before they'd undergone a security check, but they'd still taste great.

"Thanks, Bess." Julie peeked inside, then put the box on the coffee table in front of the couch where they were sitting. "And not just for the cookies. It really means a lot to me to get visitors. Sometimes I feel like everyone at Wilder must hate me for what I did. I wish there was some way I could make it up to everyone."

Bess smiled. Julie was making what she had to ask easier. "Actually, Julie, there is a way you can help some people at Wilder," she said. "Yesterday, at a rush party, Eileen O'Connor and I overhead two girls talking about this guy who could get them all the drugs they wanted. I think their connection may be the same guy who sold to you."

Some of the color drained out of Julie's cheeks, and she began fiddling with the sleeves of the long yellow sweater she wore over her jeans. "Look, Bess, if you came here to get the guy's name, forget it. I've been through enough. I don't need any more trouble in my life right now. And he's definitely trouble. Big trouble."

"I know," Bess said quietly.

"What do you mean?" Julie asked sharply. "You *know* him?"

"I realize that Dave isn't the rarest name in the world," Bess said, looking straight at Julie. "But that's the name the girls mentioned. And it happens to be the name of a guy who cornered me in his room at a Zeta party. Dave Cantera."

Bess studied Julie's face looking for some reaction to his name, but Julie didn't give her a clue that he was the one. "He was drunk, maybe stoned, and—well, it was a very close call, Julie. I really could have been date-raped."

Bess paused, hoping that Julie would say something to confirm her suspicions about Dave. But she remained mute.

"I could have reported him, but I didn't," Bess continued. "I didn't even tell my friends what happened right away. I kept telling myself nothing had really happened. And the worst part was I felt guilty when I should have been angry."

Julie still didn't say anything, but Bess could see the signs of struggle on her face.

Leaning forward, she said to Julie, "Boy, did I have it backward. I am guilty—not because I went up to Dave's room, but because I didn't turn him in. I didn't want to let what almost happened to me happen to another girl. How about you? Can you just sit back while he turns other girls on to drugs and ruins their lives? Can you, Julie?"

"No," Julie whispered so softly Bess wasn't sure she had even said it. Then Julie repeated it more forcefully, "No! What can I do to help?"

Nancy tucked her tape recorder, notebook, and half a dozen pens into her backpack. She felt adrenaline surge through her body. Being a reporter was exciting.

Casey said she would meet Nancy in the suite lounge so they wouldn't disturb their roommates, who would probably still be asleep at nine on a Saturday morning. Nancy knew that Kara wouldn't have minded, but she was relieved she wouldn't have to see Stephanie.

Nancy felt sorry for Casey, having to room with Stephanie Keats—the most annoying person in the suite. Even though Kara borrowed Nancy's things without asking, she was still preferable to Stephanie—or Bess's roommate, Leslie King..

Poor Bess!

Maybe that's why Bess wanted the car, Nancy thought, to get away from Leslie. Bess had been strangely silent that morning about her reason for needing to borrow Nancy's

Mustang. Nancy had turned over her car keys without asking any questions. Still, it was strange. Bess wasn't exactly an early riser, yet she had been up and out by eight.

Maybe, Nancy thought, she, Bess, and George could get together Sunday night after she finished her article on Casey. There had a lot of catching up to do. She hadn't told either of them a word about Peter. And after her date, there might be a lot to tell. . . .

On the drive back to Wilder, Bess felt great. She'd show George and Nancy that she could make it on her own, too. Even on just the sort of adventure that the three of them had shared more times than she could count.

Not quite on her own, though.

Julie wasn't willing to finger Dave to the authorities unless there was enough corroborative evidence to put him away for a long, long time.

Bess knew she needed someone else to help her nail Dave Cantera. Julie had been adamant about how rough and tough Dave could be— as if Bess didn't know. What she was planning to do was risky. *Very* risky.

Bess definitely needed a cohort. But who?

Nancy and George occurred to her immediately, but Nancy was working on her profile of Casey, and George was probably with Will somewhere.

Then an image of Eileen O'Connor flashed into Bess's mind. Eileen had been with Bess at the Kappa house when she'd overheard the girls' conversation about Dave. She had seemed outraged, too. Bess was sure Eileen would want to help her put Dave out of business.

Yes, the more she thought about it, the more she realized that Eileen was the best person to help her.

Dave would never believe Bess would seek him out to buy drugs. Not after what had happened between them. But he didn't know Eileen. Eileen could pretend to want to buy drugs and tape-record everything. That would be all the proof they needed.

Perfect! She'd call Eileen as soon as she got back to Wilder.

"How would you like to visit exciting downtown Springdale?" Casey asked Nancy as they hurried down the stairs from the third floor of Thayer.

"Your hometown? Great!" Nancy said. "By the way," Nancy added in a soft whisper, "did you bring the letters?"

Casey nodded as she tapped her large leather shoulder bag. "I also found my high school yearbook from when I was a freshman. That was the last year I was in a regular school. After that I was tutored on the set of

*PD*. Anyway, I saved the yearbook to remind myself what regular life was like. I thought there might be something in it to help you with your article."

"Thanks," Nancy said.

Casey looked thoughtful for a moment. "I hope I didn't freak Bess out with all that weird stuff yesterday—being followed, the hang-up calls, and the creepy letters."

"No, she's tougher than she looks. When we were in high school together, we dealt with much worse than anonymous admirers and nosy reporters," Nancy said. "And, speaking of Bess, she borrowed my car this morning. So we'll need to go in your car."

"Fine with me," Casey said as they stepped outside. "I'm always glad to be behind the wheel."

"Casey! Casey!" a man's voice called.

"Oh, no," Casey said under her breath as Gavin Michaels jogged toward them. He tripped on the curb and went flying. Nancy stifled a laugh. He really was a klutz.

"Should we try to lose him?" Nancy asked.

"Yeah!" Casey said, racing Nancy to her little white MG. She had the car started before Nancy even closed her door.

Nancy buckled her seat belt as the car zoomed out of the lot with Gavin Michaels running behind them.

"Wait! I just want to—" But his words were

drowned out by the hum of the engine as the girls drove out of the parking lot and onto the street.

"I wonder what kind of car he drives?" Casey said, almost as if she were speaking to herself.

"Why?" asked Nancy. It seemed like a strange question to ask under the circumstances.

"Several times when I've been out driving the past few weeks I've noticed a black car in my rearview mirror. I thought maybe it was him, spying on me." Casey shuddered.

"I didn't notice any black cars in the lot, but he could have parked somewhere else," Nancy pointed out. She paused, then continued on a different tack. "When you used to see Michaels in California, did he act as if he might have had more than a professional interest in you?"

"What do you mean?" asked Casey.

"I was just thinking maybe he started to develop a personal interest in you while he was writing about you," Nancy mused. "Maybe he fell for you."

"I don't think so," Casey said. "But I might not have noticed. I mean, part of being on TV is that a lot of people I never even met think they know me because they spend a half hour every week watching me on *PD*."

"That must be weird," Nancy said sympathetically.

"It is," Casey agreed. "Sometimes it's like they've been having conversations with me in their minds and assume that I know what they're talking about. I try to be polite, but not too friendly, or they may get the wrong idea." Casey was silent for a moment, thinking. "I guess it's possible, about Gavin being interested in me, but I find it hard to believe that the letters are from him."

"What else do you know about him?" Nancy pressed. She still felt that the sleazy reporter was up to something more than just researching his next article for the *Hollywood Star*.

"I called my agent last night," Casey said. "I pretended I just wanted to chat, but I really pumped her for information about Gavin Michaels. She said he's working on an unauthorized biography about me. Apparently he's talking to everyone who ever met me or says they did. She thinks it's going to be brutal."

"Why? Why doesn't he just tell the truth about your life?" Nancy said.

"The truth doesn't sell as well as a sensational lie. Contrary to public opinion, my life in Hollywood wasn't all that glamorous. Sure, I dated Charley, but most nights I was asleep by nine. I had to be at makeup by six-thirty, and some days we worked twelve or fourteen hours straight.

"Don't get me wrong, I'm not complaining. I loved doing the show. But despite what my parents thought, I wasn't out partying much. I don't drink or do drugs, so there wasn't a lot to write about me that would sell papers."

"But not everything Gavin Michaels wrote about you was a lie," Nancy said, remembering what Casey had told her yesterday.

"I know. That's the weird part. In every article there was something about me that was not only true, but very personal, like he had an inside source. Those parts scared me more than the lies."

Nancy could see why they would. Anyone could make up lies, but how could Gavin Michaels have gotten hold of the truth?

"Oh, I forgot to tell you," Nancy said. "When I caught Michaels going through the trash in the Dumpster, he had some crumpled-up papers that I bet belonged to you. Maybe he did the same thing in California—and found some things in your trash that he put in his article."

Casey shrugged. "Maybe," she said. "Speaking of trash, the letters I told you about are in a folder in the bag behind my seat."

Nancy reached back and took out a thick folder of letters. "Wow, there are a lot," she said.

"Those are just the most recent ones. I

would have to rent a U-Haul to carry all of them around with me."

Nancy flipped through the letters. They were all handwritten on plain typing paper. She pulled out one that was dated just last week.

Dearest Casey,

I dream about you every night, and we are so happy together in my dreams. You throw back your head and laugh just like you do on TV. When I wake up, it's as if you were still beside me.

I know it must be torment for you not to know who I am. I know that when you see how much I love you, you will feel the same way for me as I do for you.

But I must keep my identity a secret for a little while longer. I want to have everything perfect and ready for you. You deserve the best, and I want you have everything your heart desires.

You were wise to reject Hollywood and all the phonies there who wanted only to take advantage of you. When you came home to your own backyard, I was even more convinced than ever that you were the one for me—now and forever.

I love you.

The writer didn't sign his name—of course, Nancy didn't expect that he would. Besides, no signature was necessary—the entire letter was like a signature. The writing was distinctive. Although the script wasn't flowery, it was open and easy to read. The capital *W*'s and *H*'s were especially large.

Nancy read a few other letters, but they were all pretty much the same. They all spoke of his love for Casey and his plan for them to be together soon.

"Can I keep these?" Nancy asked.

"Be my guest. I'm not sure why I saved them. They give me the creeps."

Nancy read a few more. "Is this true?" Nancy held up the letter she was just reading. "Did you wear a pumpkin costume to your high school Halloween party?"

Casey giggled. "Yes. I even won a prize for most colorful costume."

"So, the secret letter writer could be someone who went to high school with you," Nancy reasoned.

"I guess so," Casey agreed. "I think there's a picture of me in that costume in the yearbook," Casey said.

Nancy took the yearbook out of Casey's bag and flipped through the pages. Eventually she found the picture Casey had referred to. She was standing with the other costume winners.

Casey concentrated on her driving as she steered the sports car onto the ramp to the highway that would take them to Springdale.

Minutes later they were cruising north, and she was enjoying the drive. It was a pretty day, and it was good to get off campus for a few hours. Nancy put the yearbook aside and settled back into the bucket seat of the white sports car. She took a deep breath and realized she even liked the smell of the car's old leather upholstery.

"Fabulous car," Nancy said. "And it looks as though you take really good care of it."

Casey patted the dashboard. "Oh, we take care of each other. I ought to replace the gas gauge, but I'm waiting until I can find a vintage one. Which reminds me, I should probably get some gas soon."

"Maybe I should start the interview now." Nancy leaned forward for the bag she'd put at her feet. "Let me just dig out my tape recorder first. We can get some background stuff out of the way."

Soon they were driving through Springdale, with its mixture of appealing Victorian homes and pleasant shops. There was also a miniature Silicon Valley set at a discreet distance from the more charming parts of town. It was the economic heart of Springdale, just as Wilder University was the chief employer in the town of Weston.

Nancy hit the Record button. "Tell me what you remember about growing up here," Nancy said.

As they continued their drive, Casey pointed out buildings as she spoke, "That's the house where I lived until I was three. That's the shop where my mom took me to buy my first bra— isn't that a hilarious thing to remember? There's Bertner High School, where I made my stage debut. Want to know a secret, Nancy?"

"On the record or off?" Nancy asked as Casey parked in the semicircular driveway in front of the sprawling brick school.

"Oh, on, why not?" Casey smiled. "I made my debut in *Grease!*"

"The same play you're doing at Wilder? You're kidding."

Casey rolled her window down all the way, stuck her head out, and sniffed.

"Not kidding. I think I can still smell the hair goo all the guys used. I played Rizzo, the part that Bess thinks I should have tried out for at Wilder. I told her I just wanted a small part, and that's true, but it's also true that the part of Rizzo is, well, kind of jinxed for me."

"What do you mean?" Nancy asked, intrigued. "Didn't the production go well?"

"It went fine," Casey said. "And it was definitely a turning point in my life. That's when I knew I wanted to be an actress."

Pausing, she looked at Nancy's tape recorder, as if not quite certain that she wanted her next words captured. Then she took the plunge.

"I fell in love with the guy who played opposite me. Hey, it's the story of my life, right? I didn't go quite as far with Mike as I did with Charley, but it was pretty heavy-duty. Truly, madly, deeply in love. Only he stayed behind, and I went to Hollywood."

"You sound a little wistful," Nancy prompted.

"Well, I don't miss him, if that's what you mean. I outgrew him, but I think I really hurt him," Casey said. "I was very young and all excited about my big break. I wasn't very considerate."

Folding her hands behind her head, Casey slid down and relaxed against her seat. "I mean, Charley really cares about me, but he's got a life," she said. "But Mike—I *was* his life." Casey sighed. "I don't ever want anyone to be vulnerable because of me again. Do you know what I mean?"

Nancy thought of Ned. "I think so."

Casey started the car. "So, what other sights can I show you?"

"Let's just keep driving around and talking, the way we've been doing. This is going to be a great profile, by the way."

"I know," Casey said as she pulled out of the high school parking lot back onto the main street of Springdale. "I don't know what it is about you, Nancy, but I'm giving you stuff that the most seasoned reporters on *Variety* and the *Los Angeles Times* couldn't get out of me. You—"

"Oh, no!" Nancy interrupted her. "I don't believe this! The light on my tape recorder is flashing. The battery is low."

"Well, that's easy to fix," Casey said. "We'll just go get you another."

"Not so simple, I'm afraid," Nancy replied. "It's a special minibattery. Oh, well. That's why pens and notebooks exist," she added philosophically.

"Don't worry about it," Casey said. "It gives me a chance to show off one of the seven wonders of exotic Springdale—Everything Electronic. They have more batteries than Stephanie Keats has unkind thoughts."

Nancy couldn't suppress a smile. "That's a lot of batteries," she agreed.

"Um, you might make that comment off the record," Casey said. "In the interest of peace and harmony in Suite 301."

"What comment?" Nancy asked innocently. "I didn't hear a thing."

# CHAPTER 9

*Rrrrring.*

Stephanie rolled over in bed and looked at the clock on her bedside table. It read 9:15. Who would be calling at this ungodly hour?

"Hello?" she said in a sleepy voice.

"Hi, honey, did I wake you?" At the sound of her father's voice, Stephanie was instantly awake.

"Uh, no, not really, I was—"

"Listen, sweetheart, I don't have much time. I'm calling from the airport, and they just announced that my flight will be boarding in five minutes. But I just had to call you before I left. I didn't want to leave things the way they were yesterday."

Stephanie felt a rush of love for her father.

Maybe she shouldn't have hung up on him that way. "Me, too, Daddy. I'm sorry."

"That's my girl. I feel a lot better now."

"So where are you off to? Chicago? New York? San Francisco?" Stephanie asked, naming some of the branch offices of Mr. Keats's law firm.

"Well, no, actually I'm going to Cleveland," he said.

"I didn't know you did business in Cleveland," Stephanie said, suddenly suspicious.

"This isn't a business trip. I'm going to meet Kiki's parents."

Stephanie felt her heart start to pound.

"I know this is a lot for you to absorb in a short phone call, but I wanted you to be the first to know. I proposed to Kiki, and she's accepted. We're going to visit her parents to plan the wedding."

Stephanie tried to say something. She wanted to scream into the phone. This was the worst news she had ever gotten. How could he even think of telling her this way? On the phone! He should have come to see her in person to break the news to her more gently.

"We'll talk about this later. My plane is boarding. I'll call you from Cleveland. I love you, sweetheart," he continued. "Be good. I've got to go."

Stephanie held the phone long after she had heard the click. Then she hurled it across the room. It fell onto a soft pile of clothes near the closet.

She wished it had smashed to pieces.

Nancy got a premonition of danger from the letters Casey had shown her. She wished she could agree with Casey that they were harmless, but she couldn't.

"Casey," Nancy began, "I've got to tell you, I don't think it's safe to keep those letters to yourself. You really should consider notifying campus security so they can watch out for you. Maybe even contact the local police."

"I know I should, but I can't risk my parents finding out about this. You have no idea how overprotective my folks are. If they get one whiff of this, it'll be the end of regular college life for me. I don't want to be followed around by bodyguards any more than I do by reporters or some guy who's whacko about me."

"There *is* a difference," Nancy said. "Besides," she added, "it's not just a question of your own safety. You live in a community, Casey. If this guy comes after you, you might not be the only one who gets hurt."

Casey gulped audibly. "I hadn't thought about other people. You're right, the last thing I want is to be responsible for anyone getting hurt. Even Stephanie Keats."

"Wow," Nancy said as the actress made a neat right turn into a parking lot. She was staring at a tan brick building that was only one story high but seemed to ramble on forever. "I see what you mean about Everything Electronic. It's gigantic. I— Casey! Watch out!"

Casey hit the brakes.

Shaken, Nancy pointed to the black Saab that Casey had just missed by inches. "That was a close call!"

"Sorry, Nancy," Casey said. "I was distracted by our conversation. That would have been an expensive scrape."

Casey stared at the car for a long moment, her expression unreadable.

"What is it, Casey? Are you all right?" Nancy asked.

"Mmm. I'm fine. Remember when I told you I thought I was being followed? By a black car?"

Nancy nodded.

"The car that followed me looked a lot like this one." Casey pointed to the black Saab she'd almost hit.

"It's a pretty common car," Nancy said, "but we can be on the lookout for one around the dorm."

Nancy noticed how uncomfortable Casey had become, talking about that car. She decided to change the subject. "Come on, let's get that battery so we can continue with the interview," Nancy said, leading the way into the electronics store.

\*    \*    \*

With a sigh Dawn stuffed the washing machine full of clothes. She realized that the last time she had worn some of them, she had been with Peter. Some of them still had his smell on them. She pressed a T-shirt to her face and inhaled deeply. It made her think of the times when Peter would come to her room, exhausted from working late and lie on her bed. She'd massage his neck and back till he dozed off. Then she'd lie down next to him and snuggle against him.

She tried to shake off those romantic thoughts of Peter. It was time to wash him out of her clothes, out of her life.

Bill Graham, also an RA, looked up from the detergent box he was reading. A chemistry major, he always studied the fine print on labels.

"This one's guaranteed cruelty free. Isn't that nice to know?" he said. "I'm sure my socks will be grateful."

"I think they're trying to tell you that it wasn't tested on animals," Dawn said. She adjusted the dials, then fed quarters into the machine.

"Yup, that's what it says," Bill agreed. "'Not tested on animals.'" He put the box down. "I'm just nervously making conversation," he said. "In case you hadn't noticed."

"Really?" She smiled at him. "Since when

are you nervous around me?" Dawn had always thought of Bill as a friend.

"Since you stopped dating Peter Goodwin," Bill said. He grinned. He was the sort of guy whose smiles would always be described as grins, Dawn thought. "Want to go out tonight, Dawn?"

"You and me?" She blinked. "A date?"

"Yeah," he said. "Saturday night is the traditional date night."

Staring at the porthole on the front of the washing machine, Dawn watched the sudsy waves swell and ebb.

She imagined Peter doing his laundry with Nancy Drew, the two of them laughing over the Laundromat's silly magazine collection.

She imagined all sorts of things. And then she imagined having a plain old-fashioned good time with Bill Graham on a Saturday night.

"Okay," she said. "You've got a date!"

The man stood next to the little white MG in the parking lot of Everything Electronic. Casey, you're so impulsive.

So unpredictable.

Sometimes it's hard for me to keep track of your every move.

I want to be with you every moment. And when I can't have you in my sight, I need to know where you are. To make sure you're happy and safe.

Fortunately I have just the thing—a magnetic bumper beeper. After I place it underneath your car, I can track you wherever you go.

Anytime, anywhere . . .

It's not nearly as good as being with you, my darling. But it's the next best thing—for now—till we can be together.


When Nancy walked into Everything Electronic with Casey, she could feel the air crackle around them. And it wasn't from static. The Casey Recognition Factor, she thought.

It wasn't just that Casey was a star and people were doing the usual double-takes. The red-haired actress was back in her hometown, and Nancy would have bet that half the customers and employees in the crowded emporium knew Casey personally.

Nancy found the battery she needed, paid the cashier, and caught up to Casey, who was still talking to people in the store.

"Oh, Nancy, I want you to meet my second-grade teacher, Mrs. Richards," Casey said, after hugging a slim, dark-haired woman who was shopping for a microwave oven. "And this is Nelson Dietz," she added, introducing Nancy to the tall, good-looking, mustached clerk who was helping Mrs. Richards evaluate the dozens of models. "We went to the same high school."

When they were a safe distance away, Casey whispered, "I don't believe it. Remember the guy I was telling you about, my old boyfriend, Mike, the one who played opposite me in *Grease!*? Well, Nelson Dietz was his best friend. Probably still is."

Nancy recalled some of the things Casey had told her about Mike when they'd driven around Springdale. "Do you think Mike is the one sending you the letters?" Nancy asked Casey.

"Mmm. I hadn't thought of him," Casey said. "He wrote me a few times when I first went to Hollywood, but I returned the letters without even opening them." Casey seemed embarrassed. "I really wasn't very nice to him."

"Maybe that's why he started writing you anonymously," Nancy reasoned.

"Could be. That might make sense," Casey conceded.

"Would you recognize Mike's handwriting— was it like the writing in the letters?" Nancy asked.

Casey looked thoughtful. "Well, I'm not sure. It's been a few years since I last saw anything he wrote. And in school we didn't send notes to each other very much. And we were in different grades, so I never borrowed his class papers."

"What about the letters he wrote to you in Hollywood?" Nancy asked.

"Like I said, I sent them back without opening them. I don't really remember the writing on the envelopes, I'm afraid," Casey replied.

The disappointment showed on Nancy's face. "Maybe there's some way we can get a new sample of Mike's handwriting," Nancy said, thinking out loud.

Casey was lost in thought. Finally she spoke again. "I just can't imagine Mike doing something like that. But maybe I don't know him as well as I thought I did. And people do change. I mean, I almost didn't recognize Nelson—he looks so different."

The more Nancy thought about Mike, the more likely it seemed to her that he could be the one. "Mike was really hung up on you. When he read that you were coming to Wilder—so close to home—he might really have flipped. And that would explain how the letter writer knows so much about you."

"So what are we waiting for?" Casey said. "If it is Mike, Nelson may be able to help us. Let's go back and ask Nelson about Mike."

But when the two girls got back to the microwave counter, Nelson was gone.

"Maybe he went on a break," Casey said.

"Or maybe he went to call Mike and tell him you're here." Even though Casey insisted that the letters were not threatening, Nancy decided that the actress could be in danger.

"Excuse me," Casey asked another clerk, "do you know where Nelson Dietz went?"

"I saw him carrying something out to a customer's car," the clerk said.

"Let's go," Nancy said. "Maybe we can catch him in the parking lot."

The two girls found Nelson struggling to get a large microwave into the back of a small foreign car. He seemed surprised that they were looking for him.

"Hey, Nelson. I was just wondering if you ever see Mike around," Casey said.

"No, we kind of lost touch," Nelson said.

"Well, if you do run into him, tell him hello for me," Casey said.

Nancy nudged Casey. "Is that the Mike you were telling me about?" Nancy hoped Casey would play along. She didn't want to lose this opportunity.

Casey looked puzzled but didn't blow it.

"I'd love to meet him," Nancy continued. "Maybe he and Nelson could come visit us at Wilder."

Nelson's eyes lit up at the suggestion. Casey finally caught on to what Nancy was getting at.

"Sure, that's a great idea." Casey took a pen and a piece of paper from her bag. She scribbled down her dorm phone number and passed it to Nelson. "That's my number. Why don't you try to get in touch with Mike, then give us a call. We'll all go out for pizza or something."

"Uh, sure." Nelson pocketed the piece of paper. "I will. You're looking good, Casey. It's great to see you."

"Thanks," Casey said. "Nice guy," she said to Nancy as they got into the MG. "And pretty bright, too. I'm surprised he ended up behind a counter here. I thought he might become a teacher or something."

"He looks older than you," Nancy said.

"He is. I was only a freshman when I played the lead in *Grease!* He and Mike were seniors. "I really do wonder what happened to Mike now."

So do I, Nancy thought. So do I.

# CHAPTER 10

It took Bess almost an hour to pick out her outfit for the Theta party. The Thetas dressed as wild as they partied, and Bess didn't want to attract attention to herself by being too conservative.

Unfortunately, Leslie noticed and had to make a snide remark. "Trying out a new look?" she asked taking in Bess's tight jeans and flimsy top, "Or is Kappa having a costume party?"

Bess already had butterflies in her stomach, and Leslie's comments didn't help settle it.

"Actually, I'm going to a Theta party tonight," Bess said.

"Really?" Leslie raised her eyebrows. "Taking a walk on the wild side, hmmm."

Bess wasn't about to explain her plan to Leslie. Now she regretted even mentioning where she was going. It was only because Leslie had caught her off guard.

"You look like you're going out for a change," Bess remarked as Leslie put a few more things in her backpack.

"Actually, I am," Leslie said, a superior smile on her face. "Professor Ross selected me to be his assistant for the semester. I start work Monday, and I want to move some things to my desk in the biology department, so I'm prepared for my first day."

Bess couldn't imagine a fate worse than working for Professor Ross. She was barely making it through his biology class.

But Bess was pleased to hear that Leslie had gotten the job. Maybe it would keep her out of their room more.

It was taking Bess forever to get ready to go. First her outfit, now it was taking her several minutes to apply her lipstick, because her hand kept shaking. Finally she got it right.

Get a grip, she said to herself. But it wasn't easy. Just the thought of being in the same building as Dave Cantera made her skin crawl.

At least she wouldn't have to be in the same room with him. That was Eileen's job—she was going to pose as the druggie who wanted to score to get him to talk about what he was selling.

Eileen didn't seem nervous at all about this,

and Bess hoped she was right, that there was nothing to worry about.

Bess couldn't stop worrying, though. There were only about ten million ways the whole thing could blow up in their faces. Like with her and Eileen ending up in jail. Or worse.

It's just like acting, she kept telling herself. You're not *really* buying drugs, you're just *pretending* to.

She imagined trying to convince the police of that.

"Tell it to the judge, lady."

"Mom? Dad? You're not going to believe this, but—"

As she dropped her lipstick into her shoulder bag, Bess felt the reassuring solidity of the borrowed tape recorder.

She took two deep Holly Thornton–style yoga breaths and went off to meet Eileen. They needed to go over everything one last time before the party.

Casey had dropped Nancy off at the *Wilder Times* office so she could begin to write up her interview with Casey on the paper's word processor.

In addition to her notes, Nancy had the letters from Casey's secret admirer and Casey's old high school yearbook in her bag.

Nancy had agreed to keep the letters and anonymous phone calls out of her article.

Casey was afraid that someone else might try writing copycat letters and make her life at Wilder more difficult than it was.

Nancy was worried about Casey. She hoped Mike wasn't seeking revenge against Casey for breaking up with him and returning his letters. But even though there were a lot of reasons to suspect Mike, she couldn't shake the idea that Gavin Michaels had come all the way from Hollywood to Wilder for more than just an interview. He was desperate enough to go through a Dumpster full of garbage to get dirt on Casey. Was he obsessed enough to write those letters, too?

Nancy spread the letters out in front of her. She heard the door to the office open, and she quickly tucked them into the yearbook. She didn't want to betray Casey's confidence and have the letters end up being front page news in the next issue of the *Wilder Times*.

Usually Nancy would have been pleased that one of her colleagues had shown up. She liked the energy of a busy newspaper office with everyone talking and typing. It was lonely working in the office by herself.

But this afternoon she needed to concentrate so she could get her work done quickly. She had her date with Peter, and she wanted plenty of time to get ready so she could put together a fabulous outfit. She wanted to look great. Nancy smiled at the thought of Peter's handsome face, then turned toward the door.

She was anything but pleased when she saw who had walked in.

Gavin Michaels!

"I can't believe you like anchovies, too," Bill said. He held the door for Dawn as they left the pizza place Dawn had chosen for a pre-movie snack.

"I like garlic on my pizza, too, but I got out of the habit. It interfered with my social life," Dawn quipped.

"I would think it'd take more than bad breath to keep anyone away from you," Bill said, his voice turning serious.

Dawn pulled a roll of mints from the pocket of her jeans and popped one in her mouth. "Well, I still eat these after meals just in case." She offered a mint to Bill. His hand brushed hers as he took a candy.

He seemed about to say something, but instead he popped the mint into his mouth.

Dawn couldn't help but notice that Bill wasn't his usual self that evening. Usually his pale green eyes were dancing mischievously. Now his expression was so serious.

"What's wrong, Billy boy? Why so glum?" Dawn punched him playfully on the arm. "Did one of your experiments blow up in your face today?"

Dawn knew that the boyishly handsome chem major was as serious about his work as he was about having fun. That was one reason he was such a good RA.

"Not yet," Bill said mysteriously. "But the night's still young."

He took Dawn's hand as they walked toward the movie theater.

"What are you doing here?" Nancy asked Gavin. She felt a little nervous being alone with him, especially because he was a prime suspect.

"Well, I am a journalist, and this is a newspaper office," Gavin began. He grabbed a chair on wheels and slid it over to Nancy's desk, but he didn't have a grip on it, and when he went to sit down, it slipped out from under him.

Nancy had to bite her lip to keep from laughing as the tabloid reporter's butt hit the floor.

Nancy felt herself relax a little. It was difficult to be afraid of a man who couldn't even manage to pull up a chair.

Gavin stood up with as much dignity as he could muster under the circumstances and perched himself on the edge of Nancy's desk.

"I saw Casey drop you off here. I tried to talk to her, but she brushed me off, so I came to find you," Gavin said.

"What do you want?" Nancy asked point blank.

"Well, since you're a journalist yourself, maybe you'll understand," Gavin began.

Nancy cringed at his comparing the two of them that way. She had no intention of becoming a journalist like Gavin Michaels. He represented everything that she considered bad about her chosen profession.

"I'm working on a biography of Casey. I wanted to be her official biographer, but for reasons that are not clear to me, I was denied access to her. I had already invested so much time and effort covering her career that I decided to continue with my project anyway. I still hope she'll reconsider and give me an exclusive interview, but even if she doesn't endorse my book, it will be published anyway."

"So what do you want from me?" Nancy asked.

"You know Casey. I want you to tell me about her. Where did you go today? What did you talk about?" Gavin was gazing at the papers peeking out from the Bertner yearbook on the desk. Nancy pushed it aside and covered it with some other papers.

"Well, maybe there are some things I could tell you," Nancy said. "But only on one condition."

Gavin's face brightened. "Shoot."

"I want to know your source for some of

the personal details you've printed about Casey's life."

Gavin shook his head. "As a fellow reporter you should know that the first rule of journalism is not to reveal one's sources."

"Well, then, this source has just dried up," Nancy said. She started to type, ignoring Gavin. She was gambling that he would be persistent. And if Gavin was the lovestruck letter writer, maybe she could trick him into admitting it.

Gavin sighed. "Okay, you win. I'll tell you. When I saw the pilot for *The President's Daughter,* I knew Casey was going to be a star. She was cute and funny and talented. So I started researching her life. I found out where she went to high school. I spoke to her neighbors, relatives, baby-sitters, the boy who delivered her family's newspaper. Everyone who had ever come into contact with her. It became more than a job to me; I became obsessed with her."

Nancy listened intently. He was sounding more and more like the letter writer.

"I got hold of a copy of her high school yearbook—I see you have one, too." He gestured to the corner of Nancy's desk, where she had tried to conceal it and the letters tucked inside.

So Gavin did have a yearbook. So he could have seen the picture of Casey in her pumpkin costume. The evidence seemed to be piling up against him.

"I spoke to her classmates," Gavin continued. "I even spoke to her ex-boyfriend Mike. He had a lot of interesting things to say about her. Apparently they didn't part on good terms. He was furious with her, but obviously still passionately in love with her. He seemed quite disturbed actually. He even threatened me not to get too close to her, then he begged me to give her a letter he had written to her that had been returned unopened."

Now, that's interesting, Nancy thought. She had an idea of how to prove whether or not Gavin wrote the letters that just might work. If only she could get him to write something down, she could compare it to the handwriting in the letters.

"Well, you've lived up to your part of the bargain. I'll let you interview me for your book, but not now. I have a deadline. As a fellow journalist I'm sure you understand that," she said, smiling sweetly. "But if you just write down where you're staying and your phone number, I'll call you Monday to set up a time."

She pushed a pad and pen toward him, and he eagerly jotted down the name of a motel in Weston and a phone number. Nancy had to resist the impulse to grab the pad and study the handwriting immediately. She waited till

Gavin said goodbye and closed the office door behind him.

She took out the letters and placed them next to the pad. Gavin Michaels was staying at the Weston Holiday Inn. Nancy compared his capital *W* and *H* with the large *W*'s and *H*'s in the letters.

With a sigh of disappointment she had to admit they were nothing alike.

It looked as though Gavin Michaels wasn't the mysterious letter writer after all.

# CHAPTER 11

In the smoky swirl at Theta, Bess lost sight of Eileen for a moment, and panic threatened to engulf her. It was panic city, anyway. The sorority house was crowded and jumping. Rock music blasted away over the speakers.

Eileen and Bess had been there for about half an hour, and still no sign of Dave. What if he didn't show up?

She'd be relieved, she had to admit!

But disappointed, too. Ever since she'd heard the two Thetas talking about Dave at the Kappa rush party, Bess felt determined to trap him. Part of it was motivated by her desire for revenge, she knew.

But more than that she couldn't totally relax and enjoy life at Wilder with Dave Cantera on the same campus. Ever since that night at the

Zeta frat party, Bess had felt extra weight across her shoulders. In addition to those selfish reasons, she truly believed that Wilder would be a better place for everybody without Dave Cantera.

"Dave's here," Eileen said, her pronouncement breaking into her thoughts. "The word's out. Anyone who wants to score should head for the kitchen."

"Good luck," Bess said, giving Eileen an encouraging smile.

"It's in the bag." Eileen tapped the side of her purse, which contained the tape recorder.

Bess couldn't believe how cool Eileen was to make a pun. Bess herself was so nervous she could hardly eat.

Now comes the hard part, Bess thought, reaching for another sour cream–flavored potato chip. Waiting . . .

Nancy applauded until her hands hurt. "Peter, this is fabulous!" she exclaimed as the Ten O'Clock News improv troupe took another curtain call.

"And so is your enthusiasm." He smiled appreciatively.

The houselights went up for intermission.

"I could use a cold drink," Peter said. "How about you?"

"Sounds good," she said as they got into the

concession line. "So which scene did you like best?"

"I guess the report on the breakthrough medical discovery—fake leg casts for people who want to look as though they've just had an expensive skiing vacation. How about you?"

"I liked the weather report," Nancy said. "The woman who played the falling barometer was pretty hilarious. I can't believe they just made up all that stuff on the spot. What do you suppose they do after intermission?"

"A friend of mine came last week," Peter said. "He told me that the second half of the show is even better than the first. They not only take audience suggestions for skits, they take volunteers up onstage. Maybe you'll make your debut," Peter teased. Plunking down money on the counter, he picked up two sodas and handed one to Nancy.

This was one of the best dates Nancy had ever been on. Not only because the show was so good, but being with Peter was also fun. She couldn't help but notice they way people stared at them and smiled.

Nancy knew she and Peter looked good together. She had managed to put together a really hot outfit from the clothes that Kara hadn't borrowed. And Peter wore a suit jacket over a white shirt and jeans. He looked even more handsome than usual. She definitely was standing next to the most gorgeous guy in the whole theater.

"You look like you're having a good time," Peter said.

Nancy smiled. "I am."

They were just finishing their drinks as the lights blinked, signaling that the second half of the show was about to begin.

Peter took Nancy's hand as they walked back into the theater, and it felt like the most natural thing in the world.

They sat down just as the houselights began to dim. Peter leaned over. Nancy thought he was going to whisper something to her, but instead he put his arm around the back of her seat so his hand brushed her shoulder.

"Thank you, thank you," Nancy heard one of the actors say as the applause died down. She hadn't even realized the second half of the show was starting. Reluctantly she turned her focus from Peter to the tall, balding actor on-stage.

"For our next sketch, we need a volunteer from this side of the audience, and a topic from that side. Okay, Goldilocks, you're it."

Peter nudged Nancy. "I think he means you." He stood up so she could get past him. "Break a leg!"

Getting to her feet, Nancy laughed. "Not break a leg. That was the skiing sketch."

Nancy ran up onto the stage to loud applause, led by Peter. She felt herself blush, but it was a nice feeling.

Peter had offered her an adventure, and she was having one.

Bess didn't dare breathe until she got back to her dorn. Once she was inside the main lobby, she let loose a whoop of laughter and relief and sagged into an armchair.

"You did it!" she cried triumphantly to Eileen.

"*We* did it," Eileen corrected her. "But before we celebrate, let's go upstairs and make sure the tape recorder worked and we got all of his conversation about what drugs he was selling."

Bess pulled herself out of the comfy chair. "Even if we didn't, we know where to find him. We can just go back and get him to incriminate himself again."

"I think you like living dangerously," Eileen teased her.

Bess smiled. Maybe Eileen is right, she thought. Maybe I do.

"That was great!" Dawn said as she and Bill walked out into the cool night air. "I love old movies. They're so romantic. Except for all that smoking."

"I know what you mean," Bill agreed. "I

once dated a girl who smoked. Kissing her was like licking an ashtray."

"Yuck." Dawn made a face. "I guess she didn't turn out to be the love of your life, then," she said.

Bill shook his head. "Nope. I'm still looking for Ms. Right."

Dawn got the feeling that Bill thought she might be the right girl for him. How could she tell him that as much as she liked him, it was only as a friend? It was such a cliché. But at least that didn't hurt as much as thinking that someone loved you and then finding out he didn't. Dawn realized she was thinking of Peter again.

Bill reached for Dawn's hand. His skin felt soft.

She had to tell him how she felt, and soon. She didn't want to let things go too far.

"Bill . . ." she began.

"No, don't say it. I already know," he replied. "But before you tell me you like me only as a friend, I have a favor to ask."

"Sure, anything." Dawn was relieved he had said the words she had been struggling with.

"This." He gently pulled her to him and wrapped his arms around her in a tender embrace. He looked into her eyes, asking her if it was okay.

She nodded, and his lips brushed against hers in a sweet kiss.

Dawn could feel the passion building in Bill's kiss, and she pulled away. She liked Bill, and he was cute in a boyish way. Part of her wished she felt more for him, but she didn't. The only arms she wanted wrapped around her belonged to Peter.

Bill let his arms drop, but his face was still close to hers. It was a very sweet face, and she smiled.

"Can I take that smile as encouragement?" Bill asked hopefully.

"No," Dawn answered with a laugh. Bill was too much!

"Well, you can't blame a guy for trying," he said.

"How about some ice cream?" Dawn suggested.

"Is that your way of telling me to cool it?" Bill joked.

"Come on, silly," Dawn said, breaking into a jog. "Last one there buys."

Nancy and Peter left the theater, smiling, remembering the last sketch. The entire cast had pretended to be watching a tennis match, their heads moving in perfect synchronization as an imaginary ball was hit back and forth.

They had held hands through most of the second half of the show—except when Nancy had been onstage.

Now they were still holding hands as they

walked toward the quad. It was a dark, clear night, and Nancy looked up at the sliver of moon. The stars shone even brighter with less moonlight.

Walking so close to him, hand in hand, Nancy experienced the same nerve-jangling intensity she had felt when he'd kissed her the night they accidentally fell into the lake—and into each other's arms—as she was laying a trap for the ringleader of the football betting scandal.

They both felt the passion their kiss had unleashed, but Nancy had just broken up with Ned, and Peter with Dawn. Neither one of them was ready to start a new relationship.

She shuddered remembering how scary that night had been. How relieved she had been to see Peter. How safe she had felt in his arms.

Peter slid his arm around her shoulder. "Are you cold?" he asked. "Would you like my jacket?"

Nancy shook her head.

What she really wanted was for him to kiss her.

As if he could read her mind, Peter pulled her even closer until her head was brushing his shoulder. A moment later she felt his lips on hers.

Nancy closed her eyes and felt herself transported to another time and place where there was only her and Peter, and the stars and the moon. As she lost herself in his kiss, one by one the stars exploded in front of her eyes.

She wished that moment would last forever.

Bess replayed the tape for the third time. "I can't believe it worked!" she said, ecstatic that they had the proof they needed to get Dave arrested.

"What's so difficult to believe? We had a plan, and we carried it through. We make a good team, you and I," Eileen said. "Maybe we should start our own private detective business when we graduate. O'Connor and Marvin."

Bess cleared her throat noisily. "Don't you mean Marvin and O'Connor?" she teased.

"I guess you do deserve top billing," Eileen conceded. "This was really all your idea. You figured out it was Dave, and you got the information you needed from Julie."

"Yeah, but you had the scariest part—you actually had to look Dave in the eye." Bess shuddered.

"As I said, we make a good team." Eileen smiled. "By the way, I heard that the Kappas are distributing the first group of invitations to pledge on Monday."

"Really?" Bess was nervous. What if Soozie blackballed her? Could Holly override her?

Eileen nodded. "They should be waiting for us in our campus mailboxes Monday morning."

"You sound pretty confident," Bess said.

"I do, don't I?" Eileen agreed. "That's how I hide my insecurities."

"You? Insecure? No way." Bess thought her new friend was one of the most self-confident people she knew. Everyone liked Eileen's friendly personality and good sense of humor.

Eileen shrugged. "Anyway, maybe we should call Julie and share the good news with her."

As Bess dialed Julie's number, she realized she was feeling pretty self-confident herself.

# CHAPTER 12

Nancy was up early Sunday morning. After a quick breakfast in the cafeteria, she walked to the *Wilder Times* office. She wanted to finish her profile on Casey and leave it on Gail's desk before the end of the day.

It was hard to concentrate on her work, though, with the memories of her date with Peter still fresh in her mind.

Still, Nancy knew she couldn't spend the morning daydreaming about Peter. She had work to do, and it wasn't only her profile on Casey.

Ever since her meeting the day before with Gavin Michaels, Nancy had been convinced that Casey's high school sweetheart, Mike, was the mysterious letter writer.

If Gavin had told the truth—which Nancy

140

admitted was a big *if*—Mike had never gotten over Casey. But Nancy knew she needed something that linked Mike to the letters.

Nancy settled in at her desk and began to flip through the Bertner High School yearbook. There were quite a few pictures of Casey, which was surprising because no one knew she was going to be a star back then, when she was only a freshman. Usually yearbooks focused on the graduating seniors.

Nancy lingered over a picture of Casey with a boy who had to be Mike. It was in the drama club section, and Casey and Mike were dressed up in their *Grease!* costumes. They were posing with their arms around each other in a loving embrace, but from what Casey had told her on Saturday, they weren't just acting as if they were in love.

Mike was tall and good-looking. Casey looked even younger than she did her first season on *PD*, Nancy thought, recalling the videotapes she had watched Friday.

Casey wasn't kidding about the goo the boys used in their hair! Nancy thought as she studied the boys in the background. One of them caught Nancy's eye. She almost didn't recognize him without his mustache, but it was definitely Nelson Dietz. He was a lot shorter back then. He must have had a growth spurt after high school.

Nancy started to read the autographs and

goodbye notes Casey's friends had written on the inside cover of the yearbook. There were lots of hearts and someone had drawn a picture of Casey inside a TV box. They must have known at graduation that she was on her way to Hollywood.

Nancy wanted to find Mike's inscription to compare his handwriting to that of the letter writer.

Nancy read every one of Casey's classmates goodbye notes, but there was none signed Mike. She had probably broken up with him before the yearbooks were distributed, Nancy figured. That's why he hadn't signed it.

Nancy found Mike's yearbook page. He and Nelson Dietz shared a page, and there were pictures of them separately and together. There was also a picture of Casey and Mike kissing. Underneath was written: "Sometimes you can find the best things in life in your own backyard." It must be Mike's handwriting. Nancy stared at the writing. There wasn't anything distinctive about it.

But something about that quote sparked Nancy's memory. It was a lot like something she had read in one of the letters. She took out the folder and reread several letters before she found it.

There it is, she said to herself: "When you came home to your own backyard, I was even more convinced than ever that you were the one for me—now and forever."

She compared the writing to the quote in the yearbook. Not a perfect match, but the handwriting was very similar.

That's it! There was no longer any doubt in her mind, Mike was the one. And if he was still in Springdale, Casey could be in more danger than she imagined.

"I thought Julie was coming with us," Eileen said as she and Bess walked to the campus administration office.

"She couldn't get a pass to come, so campus officials are sending someone out to Greenview to take a written statement from her," Bess explained. "If Dave's arrested and goes on trial, she'll testify against him."

"With her statement on top of ours and the tape we made, Dave should definitely be arrested," Eileen said.

An hour later it was all over. Campus officials said they'd turn the case over to the police, who would conduct an investigation. In any case, Dave would be suspended based on the tape and Julie's statement.

"Now we can celebrate," Eileen said.

"How about hot-fudge sundaes?" Bess suggested.

Eileen smiled. "The more I get to know you, Bess, the more I find we have in common," she said as the two girls linked arms and headed for the ice-cream parlor.

Casey had spent the morning at the library, and then she met her old roommate Elissa for lunch at the cafeteria.

So far it had been a good day. No one had called her Ginger, no hang-up calls, and since it was Sunday, no creepy letters would be waiting in her mailbox.

But as Casey headed back to her dorm room, she realized she was dreading seeing her new roommate. Stephanie had been especially unpleasant the day before.

Even though Casey thought she and Stephanie would never become best friends, they were stuck with each other and Casey wanted to make the best of it. She didn't like Stephanie, but she knew she was a good enough actress to fake it.

Just as Casey was getting out her key to let herself back into her room, she heard Stephanie slam the phone down. Then she heard sobs.

Should I go in or give her time alone? Casey wondered.

She didn't have to wonder for long. A moment later the door opened, and she was face-to-face with Stephanie, whose cheeks were tear-stained and whose eyes red from crying.

Without a word, Stephanie brushed by Casey to head for the bathroom.

And I thought I had problems, Casey said to herself as she tossed her backpack on her bed.

When Stephanie came back to the room a half hour later, all traces of her outburst were gone. She had even put on fresh makeup, Casey noticed.

Casey was curious what was going on with Stephanie, why she had been crying. But maybe it would be better to let Stephanie bring it up when she was ready.

"So what are your plans for the day?" Casey asked casually.

"Nothing special," Stephanie said, sounding unusually subdued. "How about you?"

"No plans," Casey said. This is like a regular conversation, Casey thought. Maybe she and Stephanie would be able to communicate after all.

"I feel like getting off campus for a while," Stephanie said.

"I know a great mall about fifteen miles south of here. All the stores there stay open late on Sundays. How about we shop till we drop?" Casey suggested.

"Your car or mine?" Stephanie asked.

"Yours," Casey said. "I forgot to get gas yesterday, and the closest gas station is in the other direction. Besides, your car has more room in the trunk for our packages."

"Ready when you are," Stephanie said, grabbing her car keys.

Kara peeked wistfully into the parking lot as Stephanie and Casey got into the silver BMW.

Hadn't it occurred to them that she was feeling kind of blue? It wasn't as if they were doing something they couldn't have included her in.

And how come everyone had an adorable car except her? Well, not quite everybody—but it felt that way. She deserved to have a car, too.

Vic had owned a great car. But his parents had taken it away when he got suspended. His weekends were even more boring and depressing than hers, she knew. But she wouldn't think about Vic. That only made her feel worse.

Well, Kara knew of one thing that would cheer her up. She'd been admiring Casey Fontaine's adorable little car since she'd moved into the dorm. She had even overheard Casey say that she would lend her car if it was important. Relieving Kara's bad mood was definitely important. And Kara knew where Casey kept her keys. She'd noticed them when she was in her room, searching for a pair of fancy sneakers to borrow.

In one seamless motion, she brushed her hair, freshened her makeup, grabbed her handy-dandy lock pick, and ran off to Casey's room to swipe her keys.

He couldn't believe his eyes.

He was eight or nine miles from Wilder, and the compass that was connected to the transmitter on Casey's car was suddenly coming to life on his dashboard.

She was heading north, away from campus, toward him!

Now the audio component was chirping to let him know that she was within a few miles and getting closer by the minute.

What was Casey doing? What was she up to? It was Sunday, and most of the stores were closed. The only place open was the twenty-four-hour supermarket—hardly a place where the rich and famous congregated.

No, she couldn't be going shopping.

Was she going to visit an old friend in Springdale?

Well, whatever she was up to, he'd find out soon enough.

He made an illegal U-turn at the next divide in the meridian strip, pulled over to the shoulder on the northbound side of the highway, and waited.

Kara loved the way the MG responded to her touch. Rolling down the window, she breathed in the cool night air. The sweet taste of freedom filled her mouth and lungs.

*Putt-putt-putt.*

Uh-oh, Kara said to herself as the little machine suddenly lurched the way a car did when it was out of gas.

But how could that be? The gauge said half full.

Kara leaned forward and patted the dashboard. "Come on. You can do it," she crooned. She pictured the gas pumps next to the twenty-four-hour supermarket. If she could just make it a few more miles—

*Putt-putt-putt.*

"Come on, little car," she urged. "You can do it."

*Putt-putt.*

"Please," she begged. "Pretty, pretty please!"

The car wasn't cooperating. Kara slammed her hand against the dashboard as the car died. She had no choice but to pull over onto the shoulder. She put on the emergency flashers.

How inconsiderate of Casey to leave her car on empty, especially if the gas gauge didn't work. Now what was she supposed to do?

To Kara's immense relief a car pulled up behind her almost immediately. So, there were a few kindhearted people left in the world after all.

Kara saw a young man get out of the driver's

side. Although it was dark, Kara could tell that the car was an import—it looked like a luxury car. Maybe the guy would be cute.

Kara checked her makeup in the rearview mirror. That's when she noticed the guy was running toward the car, and he wasn't smiling. He wasn't a good Samaritan. Now that she could see him up close, she saw the weird look in his eyes. Was he some kind of maniac?

Pumping the gas pedal frantically, Kara tried to start the car. But even as she turned the key she knew that was pointless. Confirming her fears, the engine refused to turn over.

She had to get out of there! She opened the door and struggled with her seat belt. Then a hand clamped over her mouth, and she was dragged out of the car!

# Chapter 13

Will's roommate had thoughtfully gone off to the movies. The air was full of the sound of country music and the smell of marinara sauce. It was George's idea of a perfect Sunday evening.

She came up behind Will as he poured salt into the pasta water and wrapped her arms around him.

Will put down the salt and opened the package of linguine. Slowly dropping the pasta in the boiling water, Will paused to separate the strands of linguine with a long fork.

Pushing aside his glossy black hair, George kissed the back of his neck exactly in the middle. Then Will turned around and took her into his arms.

"Honey, do you love me?"

George's heart pounded. He didn't sound as if he were joking.

"Because I love you," he went on. He said it again, in a bigger voice, as if saying it were a thrill all its own. "I love you, George Fayne."

"I love you, Will Blackfeather."

"For real?"

She looked inside herself and found no doubts. "Real as stone," she said.

I'm so lucky, she thought. Is this how Nancy and Ned used to be? I hope that Nancy finds another love. I want Nancy and Bess to feel the way I'm feeling. I want everyone to feel this way.

"It's a beautiful night," George said. "There's a new moon. You can see all the stars."

"I'd like being under the stars with you," Will said. "I've been thinking about one last camping trip before the weather turns too cold. Would you like to go with me?"

"I'd like that a lot," George answered. "Can we go fishing?"

"Of course. I'll bring two fishing rods," Will said, his hand tightening around hers. "But we don't want to be overloaded with gear. So maybe we should bring just one sleeping bag. How does that sound to you, George?"

George didn't know what to say. It sounded exciting, but scary. She knew that Will wanted their relationship to move to the next level, and she did, too, but it was such a big step. She reminded herself that she wouldn't be making that step alone. It was a step they'd take together.

George nodded her head once and answered him with a kiss.

They forgot about the pasta, and it cooked to mush.

They couldn't have cared less.

"Who are you? What are you doing in Casey's car?" He realized he was shouting and felt himself losing control.

Just when I thought I had her alone, he thought. Today was supposed to be the first day of the rest of our lives together. He was devastated and angry at the same time.

How dare this girl drive Casey's car. Pretend to be Casey.

"Where is she?" he bellowed again.

"I don't know." The girl's voice was filled with terror. Her fear sickened him.

He tossed her aside, grabbed the keys from the MG, and went back to his own car.

He'd find Casey without her help. But he wanted it to be a surprise. That was why he took the car keys. The last thing he needed was for this stupid girl to get to Casey before he did.

He couldn't wait any longer.

He had to have Casey now.
Tonight.

Stephanie turned into the Thayer lot and pulled into her favorite parking place near the front door. That way she had less distance to carry her bags. Casey was right. That mall was terrific.

She had spent far too much money, but her father was so blissed out these days he probably wouldn't even notice that the credit card bill was triple what it was supposed to be. Who was it who said that living well is the best revenge?

"Where's my car? I left it parked right here." Casey's voice betrayed how upset she was. "Do you think someone stole it?"

Stephanie looked around the lot. Casey's cute MG was nowhere in sight.

Nancy was beat. She had just finished putting the finishing touches on her profile of Casey. She knew it was her best work yet, and it was in early. Even tough-to-please Gail Gardeski would have to admit that she'd done a good job.

Although she was satisfied with her article, Nancy couldn't enjoy the sensation for too long. She had to tell Casey her suspicions about Mike. The "backyard" quote was under a picture of him and Casey together. It was also in one of the letters. That on top of all the other things she'd heard about Mike convinced Nancy that Mike was the letter writer and the one making the hang-up phone calls. And if Mike was as obsessed as Nancy thought, he might decide that being Casey's pen pal wasn't enough and come after her. She had to warn her before it was too late.

As Nancy approached the Thayer parking lot, she saw Stephanie and Casey get out of Stephanie's car. Then Casey ran to the front door while Stephanie struggled alone with too many packages.

Something's going on, Nancy thought as she took off after Casey. Casey was already through the double glass doors of Thayer by the time Nancy reached her.

"Casey, what happened?" Nancy asked. Casey was taking the stairs two at a time, and Nancy had to hustle to keep up.

"My car," Casey said on the verge of tears. "I think someone stole it."

After Nancy opened the door to the suite, they turned down the hall to Casey's room.

The phone in Casey and Stephanie's room started ringing. "If it's for me, I'm not here," Stephanie called as she entered the suite behind them. "Especially if it's my father," she added, throwing her packages down on a chair in the lounge and rummaging in her purse for her cigarettes.

Casey picked up the phone. "Hello," she said. As she listened to the person on the other end, Casey picked up a note on her desk with her free hand and glanced at it.

Nancy noticed her expression change from concern about her car to anger. She passed the note to Nancy, the phone still pressed to her ear.

Nancy recognized Kara's handwriting immediately. The note said "Borrowed your car, be back later. Kara."

Nancy shook her head. She had been pretty mad at Kara for borrowing her new leather jacket. But a vintage MG?

Nancy put the note down and listened to Casey's half of the conversation.

"No, it's not too late.... Yes, that would be fine.... Of course I do.... Okay, see you soon." She hung up. "That was weird," she said to Nancy. "That was Nelson Dietz. He got in touch with Mike, and he's coming over here to pick me up and take me to see him."

"I don't know if that's such a good idea," Nancy began. "I think Mike is the one who's been sending you those letters. I was looking through your yearbook, and there's a quote under a picture of you and Mike that matches something in one of the letters. We don't know what he'll do when he sees you."

"I appreciate your concern, Nancy, really I do," Casey said. "But if it's Mike who's doing this, I need to know why. I'm not going to be alone with him, anyway. Nelson will be there. Besides, I don't think Mike is dangerous, and he hasn't threatened me. I just want to know how he could be like this. This is important to me."

"Then let me come with you," Nancy said.

Kara was still sobbing hysterically when the state trooper pulled up behind her.

"Having some trouble, miss?" he asked, adjusting the brim of his hat. "I noticed your flashers—"

Kara threw herself into his arms. "I ran out of gas, then this man attacked me and—"

The trooper disengaged himself from Kara's grasp and held her at arm's length. "Are you all right, miss?" He handed her a clean handkerchief. "Now, why don't you calm down a bit and tell me what happened."

A few minutes later Kara had finished telling the state trooper everything that occurred.

"So you think this guy is after Casey Fontaine, the TV star?" he asked.

Kara nodded and sniffled into his handkerchief.

"Well, Wilder is only a couple of miles away. If he's over there, we'll find him." The state trooper opened the passenger door for Kara and waited till she was seated to close the door. Then he walked around to the driver's side and got in.

A few minutes later they were tearing down the highway with the lights flashing and siren blaring.

Casey opened the suite door to let Nelson in. She and Nancy were alone in the lounge. A moment before, Stephanie had stubbed out her cigarette and taken the results of her shopping spree into her room.

Nancy did a double take when she saw Nelson. His clothing was disheveled, and he looked as if he could have been in a fight.

"Are you ready?" he said impatiently to Casey, totally ignoring Nancy.

"Sure, Nelson," Casey said. "Let's go, Nancy." She turned to Nelson. "It's okay for Nancy to ride with us, isn't it? She wanted to meet Mike, too."

Casey's question had obviously caught Nelson off guard. "N-no," Nelson stammered nervously. "There's only enough room for the two of us. The backseat is full. Sorry, Nancy, maybe you can meet Mike some other time."

"That's okay," Nancy said. "I'll just follow in my car."

"Good idea," Casey said to Nelson. "That way she can drive me home later."

"Okay," Nancy said, "it's settled. I'll follow you in my car. But I don't know Springdale really well. Could you jot down the address, in case I lose you?"

Nelson grabbed a pen and pad that was next to the lounge phone, scribbled something down, and handed it to Nancy.

He's acting really weird, Nancy thought as she took the piece of paper and looked at it, West Adams and Hawthorne streets.

Something about that address was familiar. Nelson and Casey were already heading out the door.

"I'll be right there," Nancy called to Casey and Nelson. "I just want to grab a sweater. I'll meet you in the parking lot." Nancy hurried to her room and unlocked the door. She tossed her backpack on her bed and rummaged through her sweater drawer for something warm. The night had turned chilly.

She dropped Nelson's note next to the backpack and pulled on her sweater. I think I'll take the letters and the yearbook, Nancy said to herself. I have some questions I want to ask Mike when I see him.

She pulled the yearbook out of her backpack and the letters spilled out all over her bed.

Oh, no! Nancy thought. Casey and Nelson are probably already in the lot waiting for me. She started to push the letters back into the folder.

That's when she noticed the letters that had fallen next to Nelson's scribbled note. Nancy's gaze zeroed in on the distinctive capital *W*'s and *H*'s. They were the same as the writing on Nelson's note.

Nelson had written the letters!

He was the one obsessed with Casey!

And Casey was alone with him in the parking lot.

Nancy rushed to her window and saw Nelson leading Casey to his car, a black Saab. A black car—like the one Casey thought had been following her. She frantically opened the window wide, hoping she wasn't too late.

"Casey! The car! It's Nelson!"

Casey looked up at Nancy's window and then in the direction of the black Saab. Nancy saw Casey's expression change from puzzlement to one of horror, just as Nelson grabbed her.

Nancy looked around, but the lot was empty. Of all the times for no one to be around, she thought hopelessly.

Casey tried to break free of Nelson's grasp, but he was too strong. He forced her into his car.

Nancy raced out of her room. "Stephanie! Call the police! Casey's in trouble!" Nancy yelled as she charged out of the suite. She took the stairs three at a time, but it seemed like hours before she reached the parking lot.

Nancy saw flashing lights out of the corner

of her eye as she raced toward Casey and Nelson. Stephanie couldn't have called the police already, she thought. How did they get here so quickly?

Suddenly the lot was illuminated by bright lights from a police car. "Everyone freeze!"

# CHAPTER 14

It was almost midnight by the time Nancy, Casey, and Kara arrived back at the dorm from the police station.

On the way upstairs Kara apologized to Casey. "I know I should have asked you before I borrowed your car. I'm sorry, really sorry, Casey."

Nancy wondered what Casey would say. The rest of the suite was used to Kara's borrowing habits by now, but Casey had been in the suite for only a few days. And Nancy knew how she felt about her vintage MG.

"Actually, Kara," Casey began, "you really helped save my life. If you hadn't shown up with that state trooper when you did, Nelson might have succeeded in kidnapping me."

"Really? You mean it. You're not mad at me?" Kara smiled with relief.

"That's right, I'm not mad," Casey said. "But next time ask first, okay?"

"Sure thing, Casey," Kara said as they entered the suite.

They heard voices coming from Casey's room and headed that way.

"So then Nancy panicked and got hysterical," Stephanie said. "I called the police and ran downstairs to try to save Casey—" Stephanie stopped speaking abruptly when she saw the three girls standing in the doorway.

Nancy saw all her suitemates listening intently to Stephanie tell her version of what had happened.

"How did it go?" Reva asked Casey. She got up off Casey's bed and sat on the floor next to Eileen and Ginny.

Casey flopped onto her bed. She looked tired but relieved that her ordeal was over. "Okay, I guess," she said. "They arrested Nelson for attempted kidnapping."

"Did you find out where he was going to take you when he tried to kidnap you?" Ginny asked.

"That's the really creepy part. Apparently he had rented a log cabin in the woods about fifty miles outside of Springdale. It's totally secluded. He had this sick fantasy that we would live there together and be totally happy, except, of course, I would be a prisoner." Casey shivered.

"Awesome," Liz said. "I'm just glad you're all right, Casey."

Casey smiled. She was really touched by her suitemates' concern.

"Did you ever find out what happened to Mike?" Kara asked.

Casey nodded. "Nelson was in a pretty talkative mood at the station. I don't think he had any idea that what he had done was wrong. Anyway, he told the police that he and Mike had fought a lot about me. Finally they ended up not speaking at all. But Nelson was still jealous of Mike. That's why he used Mike's quote from the yearbook. He thought Mike had blown it with me and that if it had been him instead, he could have kept me happy and in his backyard—he kept using that phrase—in his backyard.

"Anyway, Mike is at college on the East Coast, studying anthropology or something like that. I got his address. I think I'll write him a note, just to tell him what happened before he reads about the trial in the paper. And also apologize about the way I acted when I broke up with him."

"Better late than never," Nancy agreed. Thinking about Casey writing to her ex-boyfriend made Nancy think of Ned. They hadn't spoken since he visited her at Wilder and they had broken up.

She realized she missed him, missed his friendship. Maybe she should write him a letter.

Ginny yawned. "I've got to get some Z's. I start my work-study tomorrow. I have to be in Professor Ross's office at eight tomorrow morning."

"I'm outta here, too," Reva said. "I have some major studying to do tomorrow to get ready for my first exams."

"Me, too," Liz said. "Good night, everyone."

Kara was still apologizing to Casey as she left to go to her own room.

Eileen followed Liz out, and a moment later only Nancy and Casey and Stephanie were left in the room.

Stephanie grabbed a pack of cigarettes off her desk and headed out to the lounge.

"Aren't you tired, too?" Casey asked Nancy.

"Exhausted," Nancy answered honestly. "But I don't think I'll be able to sleep. My head is spinning from all that happened."

"Mine, too," Casey agreed. "And I really feel like talking. This thing with Nelson brought back so many memories, about Mike and my life before *PD*."

"Do your parents know what happened?" Nancy asked.

Casey nodded. "I called them while you were giving your statement to the police. "At first they were really freaked. Mom was already on the other phone calling the airline to book a flight here, but I convinced them that I could handle things on my own. I explained how important it was for me to be more independent. Of course they weren't thrilled that I hadn't told them about the letters and the phone calls, but we agreed that the police were taking care of everything now. I think they'll come for the trial, though, which will probably be in a few months."

Casey was silent for a moment. "I should have gone to the police with those letters sooner. If it hadn't been for you . . ."

"Don't think about it," Nancy said. She could see how upset Casey was, so she decided to change the subject. "By the way, I finished my profile on you—it's on my editor's desk. I think it's really great."

"You didn't put in anything about—"

"No, nothing about Nelson or the letters. I kept all that off the record," Nancy assured her, "although I suppose everyone will hear, now that Nelson's been arrested."

"So Stephanie's warning about you wasn't true," Casey said with a smile.

Nancy bristled at the mention of Stephanie's name. "What exactly did she say?" That was just like Stephanie, thought Nancy. First she tries to sabotage my relationship with Ned. Now she wants to turn Casey against me.

"Oh, let's see," Casey began. "That you were ruthlessly ambitious, that you'd do anything for a juicy story, and that nothing was ever off the record with you."

"Sounds like Gavin Michaels," Nancy observed.

"Speaking of Gavin, I couldn't believe it when I saw him at the police station," Casey said.

"I was pretty surprised, too. I wonder how he knew what had happened. I guess he has spies or a good police band radio," Nancy reasoned.

"He cornered me in the waiting room while you were in giving your statement. At first I didn't want to talk to him, but he told me he gave a statement to the police, too. He thought he might have seen Nelson following me a few times. Actually, we had a long chat."

"You gave him an interview?" Nancy was surprised.

"It wasn't exactly an interview. We set up the ground rules before I'd give him an interview. We also talked about the biography he's writing about me."

"Is he going to stick to the truth this time?" Nancy asked.

"He said he would, but I'm not sure I can trust him. I told him that if I could review the manuscript and he incorporated my changes, I'd not only endorse his book, I might give him some special material." Casey shrugged. "He seemed excited about my offer. At least this way I have some control over what people read about me."

Nancy nodded. "He must have been thrilled."

Casey chuckled. "He was. He got so excited he bit off the end of his pencil. I think he swallowed the eraser."

Nancy started to giggle. She knew it wasn't nice to laugh at people, but she couldn't help herself. A moment later she and Casey were convulsed with laughter.

Stephanie heard the laughter coming from her room. She wondered what Nancy and Casey were talking about that was so funny. For a brief moment Stephanie wished that she hadn't left the room when she did, then maybe she would have been in on whatever joke Casey and Nancy had just shared.

Ever since her father had told her about his remarriage, Stephanie had felt very much alone, even lonely. She couldn't bring herself to confide her troubles to anyone. She had no close friends, not like Nancy, who always seemed to have a friend or two nearby.

She heard footsteps and realized that the

laughter had stopped and Nancy had stepped into the lounge.

"Well, have you done enough good deeds for the day?" Stephanie asked, grinding out her cigarette. "Or are you on your way out to look for some old lady who needs help crossing a street?"

Nancy shook her head and seemed about to head back to her room. Instead of retreating as Stephanie had expected, Nancy stopped and stared hard at her.

"Why were you telling lies about me to Casey?" Nancy demanded. Nancy's aggressiveness caught Stephanie off guard. She seemed really steamed.

"Really, Nancy, you're overreacting. I was just having a little fun." Stephanie lit another cigarette.

"Just having a little fun?" Nancy repeated. "At my expense as usual." Nancy shook her head from side to side. "I'm really sick of you and your idea of fun. What is your problem anyway?"

What's my problem? Stephanie said to herself. Suddenly the loneliness overwhelmed her, and before Stephanie realized what she was doing, she blurted out, "My father is getting remarried."

Nancy was surprised by Stephanie's unexpected outburst. Her expression softened. "My father's a widower," Nancy said quietly. "He and I are very close. I can imagine how hard this must be for you."

For a second Stephanie almost felt as if she could confide in Nancy.

Who am I kidding? Stephanie said to herself. She had no use for Nancy Drew. "Can you really imagine it?" Stephanie asked in a ruthless tone of voice. "I doubt that." She regretted divulging even that small piece of information to Nancy. She had almost treated Nancy as a friend; she would have to make sure that never happened again.

Stephanie took a last drag off her cigarette and headed for her room.

# CHAPTER 15

Bess, I can't believe you were the one who busted Dave Cantera," George said, extremely proud of her cousin.

The three friends had finally connected and agreed to meet for lunch on Monday at one of the school cafeterias.

"I didn't do it alone," Bess said modestly. "Eileen O'Connor was the one who actually got him on tape."

"Yeah, but you were the one who figured out it was Dave and convinced Julie to confirm your suspicions and carried the whole thing through," Nancy added, pleased her friend had finally put Dave and her awful experience behind her. He had been arrested and was off-campus for good.

"I guess I had a lot of practice, working with

one of the best detectives in River Heights," Bess said, smiling at Nancy.

"I'm going up to get seconds of this tabbouleh salad," George said, standing up. "Anybody want anything else?"

"No, thanks," said Nancy. "The veggie lasagna was delicious but filling."

"Don't tell me how wonderful everything tastes," Bess said as she took another spoonful of nonfat frozen yogurt. "I think I put on a few pounds from all those sorority teas. I don't know why they call them teas. They should call them sorority pig-outs."

"Speaking of sororities," Nancy began. "This morning Kara found out she was invited to pledge Pi Phi."

"Really?" George said, suddenly interested in the conversation. "I know some of the girls in that sorority. They're very committed to environmental issues. The Pi Phi members I met are in Earthworks, the environmental group I'm working with."

Nancy noticed an amused gleam in George's eyes.

"So, Kara's interested in environmental issues, huh?" George asked.

Nancy nodded. "Well, actually, she does talk about that kind of stuff a lot, like how we should eat organic foods rather than foods sprayed with pesticides. And she had a very interesting conversation one night with Ginny about dolphins and whales," Nancy replied.

George thought a minute and then looked at Nancy. "Yes, but do we think she wears only environmentally friendly clothes, say, natural fibers instead of polyester?" George asked with a mock-stern expression.

The three girls looked at each other and simultaneously burst out laughing.

"I think Kara will do just fine in Pi Phi," Nancy said, chuckling. She gave George's arm a playful nudge. "You, of all people, should commend her for wanting to be in a sorority that takes on environmental issues."

George raised her hands and arms up in the air. "Okay, I give up," she replied. "You're right. It's terrific that Kara wants to help save the earth."

"So when do you find out about Kappa?" Nancy asked Bess.

Bess smiled mysteriously as she took a pink envelope from her bag. It had Greek letters embossed on the front. She handed it to Nancy. George came back with her tabbouleh salad and looked over Nancy's shoulder as she read the note inside. It was an invitation to pledge Kappa.

"Congratulations!" Nancy said, hugging her friend across the table.

"Way to go, Bess!" George said, pumping her fist in the air.

Bess was beaming. Nancy could tell that pledging Kappa meant a lot to her.

"Enough about me," Bess said. "I saw Casey this morning on the way to class, and she gave me the short version of what happened last night. I want to hear everything!"

After Nancy had filled in all the details, Bess said, "It sounds like this Nelson guy was totally nuts."

Nancy nodded. "It's really scary when love gets out of control and turns destructive like that."

"I guess I don't have much to say on that topic," Bess said. "My love life is nonexistent. When I first met Dave, I thought he might be Mr. Right, and was I ever wrong. And then Brian—" Bess caught herself before she revealed Brian's secret. He had made her promise not to tell anyone, not even her best friends. "But speaking of love"—she turned to look at her cousin—"how's the love of your life?"

George blushed. "He's terrific," she said sincerely. Her face took on a dreamy quality, and both Nancy and Bess burst out laughing.

"What's so funny?" George demanded.

"N-nothing," Bess stammered as she tried to control her fit of giggles. "It's just that I never expected you to be the first one of us with a serious relationship in college."

Nancy silently agreed with Bess. Of the three of them, it was only Nancy who had had a serious boyfriend in high school. As attractive as George was, she never seemed to have time for dating. *I guess she just never found the right person,* Nancy thought, *until now.*

Monday afternoon Nancy was at the *Wilder Times* office. She wanted to see if Gail had read her profile on Casey and if it needed any revisions.

Gail wasn't in the office. Neither was Jake Collins, the senior editor of the *Wilder Times.* Nancy hadn't had a real conversation with Jake yet. She had met him at a few editorial meetings and admired his work for the paper. He was an excellent writer and seemed to have a knack for digging up the most interesting stories.

She hoped he'd like her profile on Casey. She'd value his opinion.

The door to the office opened.

Nancy was surprised to see Peter walk in. She hadn't seen him since Saturday night, but she had relived their kiss so many times over the past two days that it felt as if he had never left her side.

"Hi, Peter," she said, trying to keep her tone casual. She didn't want to assume that he felt as much for her as she realized she was feeling for him.

"Hi, yourself," Peter said with a big smile. He leaned down and gave Nancy a gentle kiss on the forehead. Nancy felt her heart begin to race. She reminded herself to breathe.

"I was thinking about you. I stopped by the suite to see if you were there, and Kara told me I might find you here," Peter said. "I wanted to tell you I had a really good time Saturday night." His voice was so loving and sincere that Nancy felt herself melting.

"Me, too," she said, her voice soft.

"Well, how about if we do it again sometime?" Peter smiled.

"See the same show?" Nancy joked. "I don't know...."

Peter laughed. "How about—" But he hesitated and seemed to change his mind.

There was an awkward silence. "I ran into Dawn when I was in your suite looking for you," Peter said uncomfortably. "She and I talked for a little while about my date with you."

Nancy swallowed. "Was she upset? I mean, how did she seem?"

Peter was quiet for a moment before he answered. "She was okay, I guess." He shrugged.

"Anyway, you and I will do it again, soon," Peter finally said.

Nancy nodded. "I'd like that."

"Good," he said enthusiastically. "Well, I'll call you later."

He hesitated once more.

Nancy would have sworn that he was about to kiss her again. She felt his eyes on her and anticipated his lips brushing hers in a kiss that would soon turn passionate.

" 'Bye," he suddenly said, and a moment later he was out the door.

Did I just imagine that? Nancy asked herself. It was obvious that Peter liked her, but it was just as obvious that something was holding him back. Was it Dawn? No, Nancy rejected that idea. It wasn't about Dawn. It's about us, she said to herself.

She wondered what it was.

The first face to greet Bess when she walked through the front door of Kappa house was Eileen O'Connor's.

"Bess!" she exclaimed, rushing up to give her a hug. "You were invited, too? I'm so glad!"

"Not only are we a good team, we're going to be sorority sisters," Bess said.

Bess saw Soozie turn their way. She was eavesdropping on Bess and Eileen's conversation.

"Oh, I feel a cool breeze coming this way," Eileen said.

"More like an icy wind," Bess said as she watched Soozie approach.

"Bess, I couldn't help but overhear your remark. You're *pledges,*" she reminded them. "Not every pledge is invited to join, you know."

"Soozie!" one of the Kappas called. "We need you in the kitchen."

"Just a minute," she called, and turned back to face Bess. "But it wouldn't hurt your chances of being asked to join if you persuaded Casey Fontaine to come to the pledge activities."

"You're inviting Casey to pledge?" Eileen said. She sounded a little miffed. "But she didn't rush."

Soozie smiled at Eileen. "For her, we may make an exception," she said before turning and walking toward the kitchen.

"I don't think that's fair," Eileen said. "Casey should have to rush like the rest of us."

"Oh, what does it matter?" Bess said. "Casey's a great person. It would be fun to have her in the sorority."

"That's not the point," Eileen persisted.

Bess could see this was becoming a sore subject for Eileen, and Bess was afraid that if Soozie came back and heard their conversation she would not be pleased. Bess tried to change the subject.

"How're your classes going?" she asked Eileen.

"Ugh, not great. I have an exam coming up," Eileen replied.

"Don't remind me." Bess sighed dramatically. "I haven't cracked a book in days."

"I know the feeling," Eileen agreed. "Between rush and nailing Dave Cantera, I didn't even start my art history paper on the Renaissance, and it was due today."

Bess was so wrapped up in depressing thoughts about classes that she didn't notice Holly approach.

"Congratulations, you two," she said. "I'm really glad you both decided to pledge Kappa. I think you'll fit in really well here."

"Thanks," Bess said. "But I'm not sure Soozie agrees with you."

Holly sighed. "The only person Soozie is really excited about pledging is Casey Fontaine."

Bess saw Eileen's face tighten.

"I'll do what I can," Bess said. "But I can't promise anything."

Holly smiled. "Stop worrying about it, you'll do what you can do," she said. "Don't let Soozie intimidate you."

Bess forced herself to smile. She'd try to get Casey to pledge Kappa, even though it was obvious Eileen thought it was unfair. Bess wanted to join Kappa more than anything. If getting Casey to join was the price of admission, she was ready to pay it.

\*     \*     \*

"So how was your lunch?" Will asked. They were sitting close together on the couch in Will's apartment.

"It wasn't dull, that's for sure." George filled Will in on everything. "Leave it to my best friends to have adventures."

"Did you tell them about our adventure?" Will asked.

"What adventure?" George was puzzled.

"Our camping trip. Don't tell me you forgot about it already?" Will sounded hurt.

"Of course I haven't." But George had forgotten to tell Bess and Nancy about it. Well, she didn't actually forget. It had occurred to her to mention it, but she'd changed her mind.

"So what did they say when you told them we were going away for the weekend?"

"Uh, I didn't tell them," George admitted.

"Why not?" Will asked. "You're not changing your mind about going, are you?"

"Of course not," George assured him. "It was just with so much else to talk about, we ran out of time." George knew that wasn't exactly the truth. Bess had asked about her and Will. It would have been the perfect time to tell them how their relationship was progressing. She even wanted to confide in them that she and Will would be taking a big step on their camping trip. But she didn't feel a crowded cafeteria was the place to discuss the intimate details of her love life.

"Good, because I've arranged with Andy for him to lend us some gear." Will wrapped his arms around her. "Everything's set," he said. "I can't wait."

"Me, too," George said. She shivered as Will kissed her, but it wasn't just the thrill of his lips on hers. She was nervous about the camping trip. Maybe she should have talked to Nancy and Bess about it. They always had good advice, and they would give her unconditional support on anything. But do I really want to talk about something that is so private? George asked herself.

She didn't have the answer.

**NEXT IN NANCY DREW ON CAMPUS™:**

Isn't it time Nancy came up with a big feature story for the campus paper? What exactly does fellow reporter Jake Collins want from her? Is her budding romance with Peter Goodwin about to blossom—or shrivel? And what about Ned, calling her up and bringing back such bittersweet memories? How much more complicated can Nancy's life get? Plenty. Peter's not telling her the whole truth about his past, and she wants to know why. George may take a major step with boyfriend Will, and it could spell heartbreak. And someone at Wilder has stolen a bio exam. If Nancy doesn't find out who, it could be Bess who faces failure. Nancy has her work cut out for her, but she's not about to fail the test . . . in *Tell Me the Truth,* Nancy Drew on Campus #4.

Angie Morrow had never met a boy like Jack. He was confident and gorgeous — definitely out of her league. But when he asked her to go sailing with him, well, who could say no? Maybe it was the moonlight on the water. Maybe it was them. Because before the night was over, Angie knew something truly magical was happening...

# Seventeenth Summer

**There's nothing like falling in love.**

## By Maureen Daly

### An Archway Paperback

### Published by Pocket Books

1154